GUNSMOKE

Authorized Edition based on the television series

CBS TELEVISION ENTERPRISES
A service of CBS Television

By ROBERT TURNER

Illustrated by

ROBERT L. JENNEY

WHITMAN PUBLISHING COMPANY

RACINE, WISCONSIN

"Filthy lucre! Filthy lucre!" screeches a parrot as he drops a silver coin into the outstretched hand of a fourteen-year-old boy.

Is this one of the silver dollars for which a kindly old man has been brutally murdered? And what is it doing on the property owned by Jan Gant, the boy's ex-convict father? Had Jan needed money badly enough to murder for it? And where is the rest of the money now?

It is Matt Dillon's job as Marshal of Dodge City to find the answers to these questions. He hates to think that Jan Gant did this terrible thing to an old man who befriended his family. But angry townspeople, whipped into a lynching mood by the town bully, demand that Gant be handed over to them.

Working against time, Dillon and Deputy Chester Good track down some promising clues. An unexpected turn of events, and a clever guess on Dillon's part, bring out startling and conclusive evidence. And when the gunsmoke clears, there is no doubt in anyone's mind as to who is the real culprit.

Fiction for Young People

Famous Classics

Alice in Wonderland

Fifty Famous Fairy Stories

Little Men

Robinson Crusoe

Five Little Peppers and How They Grew

Treasure Island

The Wonderful Wizard of Oz

The Three Musketeers

Robin Hood

Heidi

Little Women

Black Beauty

Huckleberry Finn

Tom Sawyer

Meet wonderful friends—in the books
that are favorites—year after year

CONTENTS

1   *Killer's Return*

On this broiling midsummer afternoon, the streets of Dodge City, Kansas, were all but deserted. Once in a while a freight wagon or a homesteader's buckboard rumbled down Front Street. A solitary figure would scuff through the wheel-rutted, scorched dust, moving from one side of the street to the other. Most people, though, avoided the brassy burning of that August sun.

In the shade of the jailhouse veranda roof, Marshal Matt Dillon and his deputy, Chester Good, sat on chairs tipped back against the wall. A bluebottle fly buzzed about Chester and he brushed it angrily away.

Dillon had the front of his Stetson pulled down over his eyes, shadowing them from the glare of the sun. He appeared to be dozing, his hands folded loosely in his lap. He was wide awake, though. The man who represented the law in Dodge did not dare snooze, not even during a hot, sleepy summer afternoon.

Chester was busy reading a small, cheaply printed booklet. Several others rested in his lap. His lips moved slightly from time to time, as he read, his high, bony forehead creased in a frown of concentration.

So engrossed was he with his reading that for a few moments he didn't get the full import of Dillon's words as he said, "Here comes Doc Adams, Chester. If you don't want to take a raggin' from ol' Doc, I'd put those kids' mail-order pamphlets out of sight."

"Uh—what say, Mr. Dillon?" Chester asked absently, continuing to read.

Then, as the meaning of the Marshal's words finally penetrated, Chester thumped his chair forward until its front legs hit the floor. He hastily fumbled the little booklets underneath him until they were partially hidden. He stared, openmouthed, toward Doc Adams as he started along the veranda toward them.

"Goodness sakes, Mr. Dillon, why didn't you say something afore this?" Chester demanded. "You think he saw them?"

"No tellin'. Doc doesn't miss much, though." Dillon

pushed his hat back on his head and grinned at Doc Adams. "Afternoon, Doc. I thought only mad dogs and Englishmen went out in the midday sun."

Doc Adams, a slightly built, middle-aged man with a straggly mustache and tired but shrewd-looking little hooded eyes, fanned himself with his hat. He loosened his string tie from his collar.

"Sure is a scorcher," he said. "Mighty glad to see the law department is wide awake and alert, standing guard over the citizenry."

Then, without warning, Doc Adams stepped toward Chester, pulled Chester's hand from on top of the partially hidden mail-order pamphlets, and yanked the little booklets out into the open.

"And Chester improving his mind, as usual, with a lot of heavy reading," Doc added.

"Now wait a minute, consarn it, Doc!" Chester almost fell from the chair, trying to reach out and grab the booklets back from Doc's hand. He didn't quite make it.

"Mr. Dillon, did you see that?" Chester's lanky figure was erect now. He hobbled toward Doc Adams, favoring his game leg, reaching to get back his booklets. Doc dodged him neatly, chuckling.

"Some folks just don't have any respect for a man's personal property," Chester protested, his thin face turning fire red.

"Oh, simmer down, Chester," Dillon told him. "Doc doesn't mean any harm. He'll give the books back to you."

Looking at the pamphlets, still chuckling, Doc Adams said, "A *man's* personal property, you say, Chester? Looks more like a child's to me. Marshal, can you imagine a grown man wasting his time reading this trash? Just listen to these titles: 'How to Be a Ventriloquist—Learn to Throw Your Voice—Amaze and Puzzle Your Friends'. . . . All right, Chester, go to it. Do it. Amaze me, Chester. Puzzle me."

Chester was now too furious to do anything but splutter wordlessly.

"And see this one, Marshal," Doc continued. " 'How to Build Strong, Powerful Muscles in Ten Easy Lessons—Be a Second Samson'. . . . Then there's one, here, Marshal, tells how to be a magician." Doc threw the little booklets down on the chair in disgust. Unseen by Chester, he winked at the Marshal.

"Matt, do you suppose the heat's got Chester, weakenin' his mind to the point where—"

"Now, Doc, you just stop that kind o' talk right this minute," Chester cut in. "Mr. Dillon, make him stop talking like that. It ain't right. He don't even give me a chance to explain where I got those little books."

"Oh, Chester, don't you know when Doc's just hoorawin' you?" Dillon laughed. "You two are worse than a couple of kids, always naggin' each other about something. . . . Doc, those aren't Chester's books. That is, he didn't send away for them."

"He was readin' 'em, though, wasn't he?"

"I got a right to pass the time o' day readin' anything I like," Chester said. "It so happens those booklets were left in the jailhouse by the last prisoner we had. I just happened to find them."

"Hold on, you two," Dillon said, then. He was peering up the street toward the Long Branch. "Looks like we might have real trouble comin' this way."

Doc Adams and Chester turned. They saw a man hurrying up the boardwalk toward the jailhouse. He was a big, hulking-shouldered man with a lumbering gait. He kept glancing fearfully over his shoulder, every two or three strides. He was gasping for breath, and perspiration was streaking through his darkly stubbled face as he stepped up onto the veranda. He turned to Matt Dillon.

"Marshal," he said, his hands working nervously at his sides, "you got to do something. You can't let him come back here. You got to run him on out o' town."

"You're pretty worked up, Galloway, aren't you?" Dillon asked.

"Sure I am." Mike Galloway sleeved sweat from his forehead. "What's that got to do with it? Don't just sit there, Marshal. Do something."

"About what?"

"About Jan Gant, that's what. I mean, who. He's back in town, Marshal. He's done got out of prison."

"Uh-huh. I'd been notified that he was released. I said, released, you'll notice. He didn't escape. Why should I bother the man? He's paid his penalty."

Galloway looked astounded. His closely set eyes widened. He excitedly waved his big, hairy hands. "Why—why, because the man's a killer, that's why, Marshal. He's goin' to kill *me,* that's why."

"I see. He say so, Galloway? He make a threat in front of witnesses?"

Galloway began to get his breath back. He looked a little sheepish. "Well, no, not exactly," he said. "Fact is, he didn't say anything. He just looked at me, Marshal. He just stood there inside the Long Branch—and, well, I ain't never seen a man look at me with murder in his eyes like that before, Marshal. The man's a cold-blooded killer, I tell you, and you've got to run him out of town before somebody gets hurt."

Dillon rose and hitched up his gun belt. Galloway was a big man, but standing, the Marshal towered over him. "Well, maybe I'd better have a talk with him, Galloway. I remember he did say something at the trial about getting you when he got out of prison, after you testified against him."

"Both me *and* old Uncle Jeff Foster, he said he was goin' to kill, Marshal," Galloway said. "Just because we done what was our duty and said we saw him draw and kill Jess Logart before Logart's hand was anyways near his gun."

Doc Adams snorted. "Sure, Gant did that. He'd have been a fool not to have done it. Logart was a professional gunny. Gant was just an awkward homesteader. If he'd waited for Logart to draw, he would've never had a chance. And Logart goaded him into the fight."

"That's right, Doc," Dillon said. "But Gant was still

technically guilty of murder. It was because of the circumstances that he got a light sentence."

"Light sentence?" Chester said, his eyes rounding. "Eight
years?"

"For killin' a man, that's a light one, Chester."

"I'm tellin' you, Marshal," Galloway cut in, "you can't
just stand here talkin'. Man like Gant makes up his mind
to kill somebody, you don't stand around talking about it.
You goin' to save me and Uncle Jeff Foster, you got to run
Gant out of town and make him never come back."

Dillon was looking past Galloway. He said, "If you
should just happen to be right, Galloway, you'd better make
tracks away from here fast, until I get a chance to talk to
Gant. He's headin' this way right now."

Galloway's head swiveled. He sucked in a harsh breath.
He grabbed hold of a porch pole and swung down onto the
dust of the street. Whispering, he said, "Run him out,
Marshal. Please!" Then he took off up the street and
disappeared into an alley a few buildings away.

The three on the porch looked at the man coming toward
them. He was a tall, rawboned man of thirty-five, with
the loose, shambling walk of a rangy hound dog. He wore
a cheap, prison-made suit, the sleeves of it so short that his

thick wrists hung out. Clumsy clodhopper shoes plodded
through the thick dust of the street. He wore no hat. His
hair was long and thick and tangled. His face, brightly
sunburned now over its former prison pallor, looked as
though the features had been cut out of granite with an ax.

Gant's was a face that looked as though it had not smiled
in a long time and might never do so again. The deeply
set eyes under beetling black brows held a haunted look.

"Great day in the mornin'!" Chester said, under his
breath. "Look at him, Doc—Mr. Dillon! I don't much
blame Galloway for bein' scared. I sure wouldn't want him
after me. You ever see a body so mean and spooky lookin'?"

"Eight years in a territorial prison will put that look on
a man, Chester. And they never completely lose it. That's
why I can nearly always tell a stranger who's done time,
when he rides into town."

Jan Gant lumbered up onto the porch and stood there,
looking straight at Marshal Dillon, his feet wide apart, his
arms dangling loosely at his sides. Sweat was pouring from
his face from walking in the searing sun. He didn't seem
to notice.

"Marshal," Gant said. His voice was deep and rumbling.
"I'm back."

"So I see. I'd heard you were free. Got any plans, Gant?"

"Yes. That's what I'm here to see you about."

"I hope they don't include trying to carry out any threats of vengeance you made at the trial."

Gant's rough-hewn face registered surprise. He waved an arm as though to dismiss the idea. "Oh, that. That was just talk, Marshal. That was eight years ago. You can forget about that. I have. Revenge loses its flavor after all that time, Marshal."

"I hope you mean that. You scared Mike Galloway out of his wits, at the Long Branch. He swears you aim to kill him."

"He's wrong. I'm not out to kill anybody." He grinned. It was just a flash of big, strong white teeth. There was little humor in it. "I reckon I just looked at him a little hard, Marshal. His guilty conscience did the rest. He knows he didn't have to make his testimony at the trial so rough against me. He did it for spite. He's always hated me—you know that."

Dillon nodded. He was remembering now that Gant was the one man in town who had ever defeated Mike Galloway in a street brawl. It had started over an insulting remark Galloway had made. Galloway, who had long been the town bully, took a bad beating. He had never regained full prestige among his cronies after that.

"How about Uncle Jeff Foster?" Dillon said.

"I was angry at him, too, at the trial," Gant admitted. "But later when I got to thinkin' on it, I realized that even though he was a friend and neighbor of mine, when he was called on to testify under oath to what he had actually seen, he had no other choice. And he did do his best not to make it look too bad for me. Then when I heard what he'd done for my wife and boy—for me, too, really, well . . . ." Gant's voice broke and his Adam's apple moved in his throat as though he was having trouble swallowing.

After a moment he said, "Marshal, how is my family?"

"Your boy, Tommy, is fine," Dillon told him. "You won't know him. He's almost a young man now, Gant. Nearly as tall as you. Fourteen, isn't he? Or close to that."

Gant nodded.

"He's a son to be proud of, Mr. Gant," Chester said. "Everybody likes Tommy Gant." He turned to Doc. "Ain't that right?"

Doc Adams was studying Gant soberly. "Yup," he said. "Fine lad. Works hard to help Uncle Jeff out at his place. Does well in school, too, I hear."

A strange expression came upon Jan Gant's face when he heard this. It looked as though he was smiling and trying not to cry at the same time. Finally, after an awkward silence, he said, "And my missus? You haven't said anything about her."

Dillon and Chester both looked at Doc Adams. Chester scuffed his foot in the dirt. Doc Adams cleared his throat and said, "I'm afraid the news isn't so good there, Gant." He held up his hand. "What I mean to say is that it *was* bad, but it's gettin' better. Mrs. Gant was a pretty sick woman for a while here, not long ago. Got real run-down. Had a bout with pneumonia. When we got her through the crisis and she was strong enough to be moved, I had to send her away for a little rest."

Gant's face showed deep concern. "She—my wife's not out at our place, Doc?"

"Uh-uh. She's stayin' with a woman I know, had some nursin' experience in hospitals back East—a Mrs. Hopkins. About twenty miles upriver, her place is. I'd planned to ride up there tomorrow, check Mrs. Gant over, and see if she's about ready to come home. If she is—and that's likely, the progress she's been makin'—I'll bring her back with me."

"Couldn't we make that trip today, Doc?" Gant asked

eagerly. "I could ride with you. I mean—well, you know how it is—I'd like to have her home with me as soon as possible."

Doc looked off into the distance, his eyes narrowing thoughtfully. Finally he said, "Could do that. But I don't advise it. Might be better if she got the extra day's rest. Meanwhile you could kind of fix the place up for her so she won't have to do much when she gets home, then ride up there with me tomorrow."

Gant thought about that. Then he nodded his head. "You know best. Who's been takin' care of the boy? Where's he been while my wife's away?"

"Over at Uncle Jeff Foster's place," Dillon said. "He's all right. Uncle Jeff takes good care of him. I've checked out there a couple of times to see how they're getting on."

"Appreciate that, Marshal," Gant said. He looked away in embarrassment. "I was wondering if you'd do me another favor."

"What's that?"

"Well, I'm ridin' out right now to see the boy and I thought maybe you'd come along with me."

Dillon looked surprised. He tapped his chest with a forefinger. "You want *me* to go out there with you? Why,

Gant? You expecting trouble with Uncle Jeff?"

"No, sir. Truth is, I'm worried about the boy, Marshal. I mean, I don't know just how he's going to take to his jailbird father coming back. If he isn't too bitter against me, I've been hoping maybe to take up right where we left off. I'd like him to know I just want to settle down to being a decent citizen once again. That's all in the world I want out of life now, Marshal. But maybe the boy'll have trouble believin' that, right off."

"What good will my being with you do?" Dillon asked.

"Well," Gant shifted his feet awkwardly, his eyes pleading with Dillon, "you could sort of give me some moral support. If the boy sees me with you and you actin' friendly like, maybe he'll get the idea he doesn't have to be too ashamed of me. He could figure that a man can come out of prison and still be in good standing with somebody of importance. I'd powerfully appreciate it if you'd do that, Marshal."

Dillon looked around at Chester and Doc. Doc nodded his head slightly. Dillon took a deep breath. "All right, Gant," he said. "Chester, you take care of things until I get back. Won't be long."

A few moments later, Dillon picked up his big roan

gelding from the livery and rode down to join Gant who had hitched his mount outside the Long Branch. As he rode near, Dillon saw that Jan Gant was talking to another man, a squat-looking but powerfully built individual with a tough, bulldog face. It appeared to Dillon that the two were arguing about something. Just before he reached them, both men looked his way. Gant spoke low and heatedly, then, to the other man. After a moment the stocky man grinned, showing a flash of gold teeth in the sunlight, shrugged, and ambled back inside the Long Branch.

As Dillon rode up beside Gant, he said, "I didn't seem to recognize your friend. Stranger in town?"

"Yuh," Gant said, avoiding Dillon's eyes. "Won't be here long. Just passin' through."

"Known him long?"

"Quite some time." Gant sleeved his face. "Sure hot, isn't it?"

"We were still talking about your friend," Dillon said. "Who is he, Gant?"

Gant shrugged. His voice showed a touch of anger now. "I told you before—just someone I know slightly. It's not important who he is."

"Maybe it could be, Gant. It could be possible you know that man from your days in the pen."

Gant turned angrily. "If so, it's my business, Marshal. Let's forget it. Huggins isn't goin' to be in town any length of time."

"I hope you're right, Gant. A man's known sometimes by the company he keeps. What was this Huggins sent away for?"

Gant didn't answer. He sat his saddle stiffly, almost bristling with anger now.

"Gant," Dillon said softly, "I'm not tryin' to ride you. You ought to know me better than that. It's my job as a law enforcement officer to find out as much as possible about strangers like Huggins. He minds his business and rides on without causing any trouble, I'm not going to bother him.... Did he pass through Dodge just to see you?"

"No. He just happened to run into me."

"You didn't seem to be having a particularly happy reunion, Gant. Weren't too glad to see him, were you?"

"Naturally not. I don't like to be reminded of the time I spent behind bars. If you must know, Marshal, he wanted to spend the night at my place. I told him No. I don't want men like him around my boy."

"You did right, of course, Gant. I could be wrong, but I didn't particularly like the looks of Huggins. Somethin' about the set of his sails hit me wrong. Well, don't worry about it. If you told him to leave you alone, he probably will."

2   *Reunion*

For the rest of the ride out to the river bottom country where Gant and Foster and other homesteaders had settled, neither Marshal Dillon nor Jan Gant spoke much. But as they neared the Foster place, Gant showed signs of increasing nervousness. Once he reined in momentarily. His face taut with worry, his eyes pained, he said, "Marshal, I'm scared. I been thinkin'—suppose the boy just refuses, sort of, to take me back. Suppose he's scared of me, even. What'll I do, Marshal? What'll I say to him?"

Dillon sighed, blowing breath up over his perspiring face. "I can understand how it's frettin' you. But when the time comes, you'll say the right things, Gant. You'll see. Kids understand things a lot better'n most grownups give 'em credit for doing. Try to calm yourself and let's ride on now."

They did that, riding silently again for several miles

before they came in sight of the Foster place.

The homestead had a neatly railed-in yard, with a dozen chickens busily pecking around. Several horses lazed inside a peeled-pole corral. On the other side of the house on a gentle slope of pasture, two milch cows grazed. In the fields behind the house, acres of grain waved gently in the soft summer wind.

As Dillon and Gant rode up, a man and boy moved from the barn area. The boy held a pitchfork in one hand. His linsey-woolsey shirt was black-stained with perspiration. As they rode closer, Dillon saw that the boy was a lot like his father, already grown tall and rangy-shouldered, with lean hips and long legs. His face held the same gauntness but was softer; it had not yet been carved by hardship and sorrow. Yet there was a certain look of maturity about the boy, Dillon saw, for a lad of fourteen. He thought of how difficult it must have been for Tommy Gant, trying to take his father's place in helping his mother to eke a living out of this tough prairie land.

Gant's voice broke into Dillon's reverie. "Look at him, Marshal," he said softly. "Look at that Tommy, will you? Grown big as a colt, he has." There was pride in his voice.

"Sure has," Dillon said.

As they entered the yard, Uncle Jeff Foster waved an arm lazily. He called out, "Marshal! Haven't seen you in a prairie dog's age. How ya be? Who's that with you?"

"Uncle Jeff," Dillon said, "you've got company. Don't you recognize your next door neighbor?"

Foster was in his sixties, yet looked as robust as a man of forty. He was short but thick-bodied and heavy of shoulder. His stout legs under their black hickory pants were slightly bowed. His hair blew in the wind, long and white and silky as a mane. His tanned cheeks were flushed with health. His long, flowing white mustache somehow took away from the almost comical largeness of his nose, which was always red and shiny and peeling a little from too much sun.

He stopped dead in his tracks and stared, his mouth a perfect O under the white mustache, as he gaped at Jan Gant.

"Glory be!" Foster said. "I can't hardly believe my eyes. Howdy there, Jan. You're a welcome sight to see."

Without looking around, he reached out a hand to the boy who had moved up behind him. He waggled his fingers impatiently. "Tommy, look who we've got here."

The boy moved up beside him, his eyes squinting against

the flame-ball brightness of the afternoon sun. "I don't reckon I'm acquainted, Uncle Jeff."

His voice sounding choked, Jan Gant said softly, "That's understandable, son. I've been away a long time."

Marshal Dillon stood to one side, watching.

Foster threw a heavy arm about the boy's shoulder. "Tommy, this is your father. He's come home to stay. I told you he would. Ain't that right, Jan?"

Gant nodded, intently watching his son's reaction.

Red flushed under the boy's dark tan. He backed away a step and averted his eyes. He wiped his hands up and down the flats of his thighs. "Oh," he said. Then he just stood there, sort of looking past the big man who was his father, as though he was afraid to look straight at him.

"It's mighty fine to see you again, son," Jan Gant said. He stepped toward the boy and thrust out his hand.

Tommy Gant stepped forward hesitantly and shook hands. "Yes, sir," he said. He glanced quickly toward Marshal Dillon, then away.

"Tommy," Dillon said. "I rode out here with your pa because there's something I think I ought to tell you. He's paid his debt to society, Tommy. He's starting over with a clean slate. He aims to keep it that way and try to be a better man, even, than before he went away. Just because a man makes a mistake, folks don't stay down on him forever. I'm hopin' that with your help, Tommy, and your mother's, your father will be a man we'll all be proud to know again in Dodge."

The boy didn't answer. He kept looking down at the ground and picking at a loose thread on his trousers.

Jan Gant said huskily, "Thank you, Marshal."

Uncle Jeff Foster coughed in embarrassment and said, "Well, dad-blast-it, don't let's all of us just stand here in this pesky sun like a bunch o' hens on a hot griddle. Let's head for the house. I got me some lemonade in the cooler."

"Sounds good to me," Dillon said.

Protected by huge shade trees, the interior of the house was a cool relief from the outside heat. Dillon swung a barrel-keg chair out from the table and straddled his long legs over it. Across the table, Jan Gant sat stiffly, awkwardly, his great hands laced too tightly together in front of him. He was watching Tommy, who stood now at the far side of the room, near a large wicker cage that held a solemn-looking, sleepy-eyed green parrot. As Tommy spoke softly to the bird, it made cawing noises.

"How long has Uncle Jeff had that bird, Tommy?"

Jan Gant asked, relaxing a bit as he watched them.

"It's my parrot, sir. I just brought him over here to stay with me."

"Where did you get him?"

"Ma bought him for me, from a drummer passing through."

"Does he talk, son?"

"Not much, sir. But he does say a few things. Would you like to hear him?"

"Sure thing, son."

The boy dug into his trousers pocket and took out a coin. He held it between his thumb and forefinger and pushed it through the cage.

"What's this, Pluto?" Tommy said. "What have I got here?"

The parrot stretched its neck, taking the coin in its beak. Then with a brisk toss of its head, it threw the coin out of the cage. Tommy deftly caught it as the parrot said, "Filthy lucre! Filthy lucre! The root of all evil! The root of all evil!"

Dillon and Jan Gant laughed. Tommy looked pleased but a little embarrassed. "That's pretty clever, Tommy," Dillon said. "You teach him that trick?"

"No, sir," Tommy said. "He already knew it. I discovered it by accident. That's about all he does say, though. At least, distinctly."

Just then, Uncle Jeff Foster came in with a moisture-dewed pitcher and some glasses. He poured the lemonade and they all sat around the table making small talk, while they drank. After a while, Uncle Jeff Foster coughed and said, "Tommy, why don't you and your pa go on over to your own place? He'd probably like to take a look around to see how we been keepin' things up over there while he was away. I won't be needin' any more help here the rest of the day."

Tommy looked hesitantly at his father. "If you'd like, sir."

"I think it's a fine idea." Jan Gant stood up. He looked like a man who had just been given a million dollars in gold. For a moment his big-featured, craggy face was softened with happiness.

Dillon and Uncle Jeff Foster watched them go toward the door. When they had gone out, Foster said, stroking his white mustache thoughtfully. "It's good Jan's come back, Marshal. The boy needs him. Nobody can take the place of a real father."

"From what I hear, you've done a pretty good job of tryin'."

"I did my best but it ain't the same." Foster sighed. "Tell you the truth, Marshal, I'm kind of glad it's over. Lot o' responsibility, watchin' out for a boy Tommy's age."

Dillon chuckled. "Don't tell me that, you old fraud. You loved every minute of it. You're as much of a younker as Tommy. I was watching that afternoon you were helpin' him break that broomtail bronc. Got thrown a couple of times yourself before you realized there's an age when a man can't any longer go in for that kind of nonsense."

The old man laughed and ruefully rubbed one hip. "I'll tell you the truth, Marshal. I was sore as a mule-kicked coyote for a week after that tomfoolery."

For a moment, then, neither man spoke. It was Foster who finally broke the silence, his voice serious now. "Marshal," he said, "you reckon Jan Gant's goin' to be—well, you know—all right now?"

"What do you mean?"

"You know danged well what I mean, Marshal."

Dillon drummed the table with his finger tips and drained the last of the lemonade out of his glass, before he answered, "I hope so. I sure hope so, Uncle Jeff."

"And what does that mean?"

"It means there just isn't any way of tellin' about a man who's put in time in the pen, Uncle Jeff. Some men it straightens out for the rest of their days. Others it makes mean and bitter and they learn some wrong ways they might otherwise have never learned—and take up with some bad company they might otherwise have never met."

When he said that, Dillon was thinking of the man, Huggins, who had been talking secretively with Jan Gant.

"Only time will tell about Gant, Uncle Jeff," he concluded. "With a friend and neighbor like you and a son like Tommy, though, he's got every good reason to walk the straight and narrow—I'll say that."

He got up from the table, picked up his hat. "Now I got to be gettin' back into town before Chester gets himself into some kind of mischief. Sure do appreciate your hospitality, Uncle Jeff. See you again."

"Enjoyed havin' you, Marshal. Don't be such a stranger out this way." Uncle Jeff Foster walked out the door and into the yard with Dillon. . . .

Jan Gant and his son, Tommy, stood by a section of drift fence, leaning against it, looking back over the rolling ground of their own homestead. After a moment Jan Gant said, "The old place looks real fine, Tommy. I'm right proud of the way you and your ma have kept it up."

"We couldn't have done it without Uncle Jeff's help," Tommy said. "It was mighty hard on Ma too. Doc Adams said it was because she'd overworked herself so much that she got so sick."

"I know. I've got a lot to make up to your ma, Tommy. To you too. . . . Y'know, Doc Adams says she can come home tomorrow, your ma. We'll all be together again, then."

When Tommy didn't say anything, Gant stepped around in front of him and took the boy's arms in his hands. He said, "I'm sorry, Tommy. I reckon I'm tryin' to pin you down too suddenlike, tryin' to rush things between us. I shouldn't expect things to go right back to bein' the same as they were before I went away. I know that, but for a moment I just wanted it to be that way so bad, I forgot that it'll take a little time for us to get to know each other again."

Tommy took his lower lip between his teeth and still didn't answer. Jan Gant forced a smile and slapped Tommy playfully on the arms.

"All right, son," he said. "That's enough of that kind

of talk. Now let's get up to the barn and have a look at some of that harness you said was in need of mending."

Silently Tommy followed his father toward the barn area.

Later, after dinner, Tommy and his father remained at the table and the boy watched his father fill and light a battered old pipe, then lean back contentedly in a cloud of blue smoke. After a moment, Gant said, "Son, don't be ashamed to ask questions. I reckon you've got some on your mind. That's only natural. Maybe it'll help us both if you bring things out into the open."

Tommy set his knife and fork together on his empty plate. He said, almost too quickly, "There isn't anything, sir."

Jan Gant smiled slightly. "That's hard for me to believe. If I was in your place, I'd have some questions."

"Like what, sir?"

"Well . . . ." Gant puffed thoughtfully on his pipe. "I might wonder, if my father made a bad mistake once, whether he might not be liable to make it again."

Tommy looked a little surprised and then quickly turned his eyes away.

"You see, son," Gant said, "I've thought a lot about you

and what it'd be like for me to come back. I reckoned it'd be a lot harder for you than for me."

When Tommy didn't say anything, Gant went on, "Nothing like that'll happen again, son. Eight years ago I was a fool, Tommy. I had never learned to control myself. I didn't think it was important. I've learned different. I had to."

Suddenly Tommy leaned across the table toward his father. His eyes bright with curiosity, he blurted, "Pa, what really happened way back then—between you and Jess Logart, I mean? I—well—I've heard lots of different things."

"Reckon you have, son." Gant puffed on his pipe. He sighed. "Well, it's not a pretty story. But looks like you might have a right to hear it. . . . Jess Logart was a man nobody liked. He was mighty handy with a gun, and because of this, people were afraid of him. He had a big mouth and he liked to show his power by insulting people and getting away with it. Anyhow, that day he took a notion to ride me. I put up with it a long time and then all at once my temper got the best of me and I sassed him back."

"Well, he was askin' for it, wasn't he?"

"Yes, Tommy, but that wasn't any excuse for me. I should have known enough as soon as Logart started to ride me, to have left the place. It would have just meant swallowin' a little pride. Sometimes that's the best thing to do, if nothing really important is connected with it—and there wasn't, really. Well, once I answered Logart back, I was in for it. That was just what he was waiting for. That gave him a real excuse to pick on me. First thing I knew, he was goading me into a gun fight and there was no way out of it. When I realized that this had happened, I got skitterish. I knew I was goin' to die, that I didn't have a chance against a man with Logart's gun-savvy. Because I didn't want to die—even if it meant killing Logart to save my own hide—I made a mistake. I didn't wait for Logart to go for his gun. Thinking back on it later, I realize now that Logart was only reaching for cigarette makin's in his shirt pocket, when he moved his right hand. But I thought he was goin' for his gun. I didn't wait to see. I drew and shot him, Tommy. I couldn't call it self-defense, son, because Logart's hand wasn't anywhere near his gun when I fired. The fact that he hadn't been quite ready for the gun fight, and was planning to ride me a little longer, didn't matter."

"Golly!" Tommy said, his eyes large with wonder. "But if Logart killed a lot of other men and everybody hated him anyhow, what difference did it make?"

"At one time, not much, son. But there's law out here now. There are still killin's. But unless a man kills in self-defense now, he pays for it—it's a crime. And it doesn't matter much who the man is he kills."

For a while after that, Tommy was silent. Then he said, "Pa, a lot of people say bein' in prison changes a man. They say he's not ever much good after that. I—well—I've heard talk that some of the other homesteaders don't like the idea of a man comin' out of prison and comin' back here to live again."

Gant's face hardened as he tapped out his pipe. "They're right about one thing, Tommy. Prison changes a man, it's true—either for better or for worse. I can't make people like having me back. All I can do is let time prove that they're wrong. We'll both probably have to listen to a lot of talk, son, for a while. It's—it's goin' to be mighty rough on both of us. Probably more so on you than me. . . . Do you think you can take it?"

Tommy Gant thought about it. Then he looked at his father long and levelly. Finally he said, a little doubtfully,

"Yes, sir. I—I reckon so. I'll try, anyhow."

Gant stood up. He moved around the table and ruffled Tommy's hair. "That's all I can ask. And I won't let you down. You'll see. . . . Now, let's get these dishes done and clean up the kitchen a mite and then hit for bed. We've got to be up early in the morning to ride out with Doc Adams to bring your mother home."

"Yes, sir," Tommy said.

About that time, in Dodge City, Marshal Matt Dillon was making his first rounds of the evening. As he passed the Long Branch, Mike Galloway came out and called, "Marshal! Hold on there. I want to have a word with you."

Dillon waited for the other man to cross the plank walk and join him.

"What's on your mind, Galloway?"

Galloway drew himself up, narrowing his bloodshot eyes belligerently. He set his hands solidly on his hips.

"Plenty's on my mind, Marshal. I been hearin' rumors around town that I don't like."

Dillon smiled. "If they're only rumors, why pay any attention? What kind of rumors, Galloway?"

"I hear you not only didn't run that murderin' convict,

Gant, out of town, Marshal, but that you actually escorted him out to Jeff Foster's place like he was—well—like some visitin' dignitary, or somethin'. That true, Marshal?"

"I rode out to the Foster place with Gant, yes. I had a reason."

Galloway shook his head in disbelief. His face reddened with increased anger. "Since when does the law in this town take to mollycoddlin' killers?"

"Galloway," Dillon's voice took on a steel-edged softness, "where I ride and whom I ride with happens to be none of your business. . . . Now if you've got nothing else to say, get out of my way."

Galloway stepped backward, an ugly sneer on his face. "That's right, Marshal, get tough with me. Push decent citizens like me around while you coddle convicted killers."

Dillon started to walk on, then abruptly turned back. He said, "Listen, Galloway, I don't know why I'm wasting time trying to talk to you but maybe I can get something into that stubborn brain of yours. Jan Gant is a land owner and a man with a family. He made a mistake but he's paid for it. Unless he gets out of line again I have to treat him like any other man. . . . And, mister, you listen to me: You'd better do the same. If you go out of your way to start

any trouble with Gant—or *for* him—you'll answer to me personally. Have you got that straight?"

"Oh, yes, Marshal," Galloway said. "I got it, all right. Only you got things a little backward, haven't you? It won't be *me*, startin' any trouble. It wasn't *me* who swore vengeance on *him*, Marshal. It wasn't *me* who said he'd kill old Uncle Jeff Foster when he got out of prison, either. And it ain't *me* who's got a hardcase friend, just blew into town and braggin' about spendin' some time visitin' with his ol' friend, Gant."

"What's that? Who're you talking about, Galloway? A man named Huggins?"

Galloway's heavy brows were lifted in surprise. "Oh, you know about him, eh, Marshal? Well, if you're any judge of character, you sure can tell there's a man ain't up to no special good. What's he here for, Marshal? What do you figger him and Gant have in mind?"

Dillon didn't say anything.

"I know one thing, Marshal, I'm sure glad *I* don't live as close to the Gant place as old Uncle Jeff Foster, with a man like Huggins staying out there with Gant."

"Where did you see this Huggins last, Galloway?"

"Why, in the Long Branch, Marshal. But he left there.

What you figurin' to do with him, Marshal? Like Gant, he ain't hurt nobody—*yet*."

"I'll find out what Huggins' business around Dodge is. I'll have a talk with him."

"You're sure doin' a lot of talkin', Marshal . . . but not very much doin'."

Dillon fought hard to control his temper. "I do my job the way I think best, Galloway."

"Hmmmph!" Galloway snorted disdainfully. "Seems to me your job is to prevent violence before it happens. Seems to me the way to do that would be to run off any vicious characters who come into town *before* they can cause any trouble."

"You're right, Galloway." Dillon forced a patient smile. "And I do that, once I'm sure they're planning trouble."

He turned and strode off. During the next hour, Marshal Dillon stopped in every likely place he thought he might find the man called Huggins. The search was in vain. He didn't find him.

3   *Doom at Dawn*

Tommy Gant awoke the next morning with only a vague
awareness that this day was somehow going to be different
from others. Then his mind threw off the cloudiness of
sleep and he remembered why that was. His father was
home.

Yawning and stretching, he kicked off the covers and
thought about that. His father's return wasn't much like
Tommy had expected it to be. During the last few years
when he had thought about his father, and talked with his
mother about him, Tommy had pictured a younger, happier
man, the kind of man his father had been when Tommy
was so much smaller.

It had been something of a shock to Tommy when he
first saw his father, and later when they had talked together.
It seemed hard to get it through his mind that the big,

grim-faced stranger who rode up to the Foster place with
Marshal Dillon was his father.

Then Tommy told himself that he was thinking like a
child. Naturally, his father would be changed. He was
eight years older, for one thing, and that changed a man.
Eight years had changed Tommy too. And spending all
that time in prison certainly wouldn't make a man jolly
and happy-go-lucky.

As his father had told him, it was just going to take a
little time for them to get used to each other again.

Now, as he got up from the bed, Tommy told himself
that he was going to have to do everything possible to make
his father feel welcome—to help him to make a new start
in life. Tommy figured that he hadn't done a good job of
that the night before. He would have to do better today. It
would probably be easier after Mom was home. He remembered, then, that they were supposed to ride out and get
her this morning.

Tommy looked toward the bed at the other side of the
room where his father had slept. The bedclothes were in
disarray but the bed was empty. His father was already up
and about.

Tommy sniffed the air, expecting to smell bacon and

grits frying on the cookstove out in the kitchen. But there was no such aroma. And the house was strangely silent. Tommy put on his clothes and went out into the kitchen. There was nobody there. There was no sign of breakfast being made.

A feeling of uneasiness came over Tommy, then a moment of panic at finding himself alone. For an instant he wondered if he had only dreamed about his father coming home. Then he saw the pipe on the table, where it had been left the night before. He grinned at his fears.

Aloud, he said, "He's probably out doing some early morning chores. Or perhaps he's gone down to Uncle Jeff Foster's to see about borrowing Uncle Jeff's new big two-man saw." Tommy remembered that his father had said they would need it to cut down timber to build new fencing as soon as possible.

Out in the back yard, Tommy crossed to the barn area, looking for his father. He wasn't there. Neither was his father's horse. Tommy was sure, then, that he had gone down to the Foster place. He saddled his own roan colt, then rode out to the trail and turned toward the Foster place. Halfway there, he noticed several horses hitched at the rail in Uncle Jeff's front yard. At this early hour that was most unusual. He urged his mount into a gallop.

As Tommy rode on, old Caleb Weems, a homesteader who lived on the other side of the Foster place, came out of Foster's front door. He saw Tommy riding into the yard and turned and darted back inside. A moment later, as Tommy dismounted and hitched the roan at the rail alongside the other horses, Weems came out of the house again. This time he was accompanied by Marshal Dillon and Chester Good. All three stood there, frowning, as Tommy walked toward them.

"What's the matter?" Tommy called. "Is something wrong, Marshal? Nothing's happened to Uncle Jeff, has it?"

Dillon stepped forward. "Tommy, where's your father?" he said.

Tommy looked from him to Chester and then back to Dillon. "I—well, isn't he here? I thought he'd ridden down here."

"He's not here, Tommy," Dillon said. "You mean he isn't up at your place?"

"No, sir. I looked. I'm pretty sure because his horse wasn't in the barn. I—I don't understand, Marshal. If he isn't here, where could he have gone? Maybe he rode on into town. Or maybe he went to get Mom."

Dillon shook his head. "No, Tommy. We'd have met him on the way out here. I'm afraid that isn't the answer."

Tommy began to be afraid. He could sense that something was terribly wrong. "How come you're out here so early in the morning, Marshal? Something—something *has* happened to Uncle Jeff, hasn't it? Where is he?"

"Now, calm down, Tommy. I'll have to ask you to answer a few questions for me. Why do you think something's happened to Uncle Jeff? You have any reason for suspecting it might?"

"Well—no, but—well—you're out here and I—I just know it has, that's all. Hasn't it?"

"I'm afraid so, Tommy. I might as well tell it to you straight, son. Uncle Jeff is dead."

"What? Oh, no, Marshal! That can't be. Why, he—I mean, he wasn't even sick. Uncle Jeff was just as healthy as he could be."

Marshal Dillon sighed and looked away. "He didn't die, Tommy. He was killed."

"Killed?" All color drained from Tommy's face. His knees felt weak and for a moment he thought he was going to faint or perhaps get sick to his stomach. "Oh, no," he said. "There must be some mistake. Who'd want to kill Uncle Jeff?"

"We don't know yet, Tommy."

"But whoever it was," Caleb Weems said, in a piping, thin voice, "he's gettin' farther and farther away while we stand here talkin' about it." Weems's beady, black little eyes, set in a face like a wrinkled walnut, stared meaningly at Marshal Dillon.

Dillon turned to him. He didn't say anything to Weems. He just kept looking at him. After a few moments, Weems's gaze shifted away. He stuck a straw between his toothless gums and sucked noisily around it.

"Didn't mean no harm, Marshal," he said apologetically. "Just makin' a suggestion."

Tommy Gant heard hardly any of this. He was trying to grasp fully the meaning of the thing Marshal Dillon said had happened. It just didn't seem possible. He would have to see for himself. He started past Marshal Dillon, toward the house.

He had taken only one step when Dillon's big hand reached out and gently but firmly took hold of his arm.

Tommy twisted his head. He was having trouble holding back tears. "Please, Marshal," he pleaded. "Let go. I've got to go in there. I've got to see Uncle Jeff. Maybe—maybe he isn't really dead, Marshal, but just hurt bad. Let me go. Let me go see Uncle Jeff."

Dillon didn't loosen his grip. He shook his head. "Uh-uh, Tommy. I don't think you want to do that. You don't want to see Uncle Jeff the way he is. He was hit hard over the head, Tommy. Whoever did it wasn't taking any chances Uncle Jeff would survive the blow. And there just isn't anything you can do for him, Tommy. He's dead all right. Doc Adams doesn't make mistakes about things like that."

Tommy stopped struggling and Dillon freed his arm. "Doc Adams?" Tommy said. "He—he's in there?"

Dillon nodded. "Caleb Weems was going into town early this morning, Tommy, and he stopped by here to see if Uncle Jeff needed anything brought back. Weems always did that. Seems that if he fetched anything back for Uncle Jeff, he got a dollar for his trouble. Anyhow, Tommy, when Weems got here this morning, he found the door open. He went on in and found Uncle Jeff in there—dead."

Tommy didn't say anything. Tears were fogging his eyes now; he couldn't hold them back. He brushed at them angrily with the backs of his hands.

"It's all right, Tommy," Dillon told him. "Don't be ashamed to cry. There are some times when nearly all men cry. They just have to."

"But, Marshal," Tommy said thickly, through his tears, "he was so good! Uncle Jeff was such a kind, good man, who never hurt anybody in his whole life."

"I know."

"He always *helped* everybody. It—it's not fair, Marshal, that he should be dead. Why, Marshal? Why would anyone want to kill Uncle Jeff?"

"It looks as though they did it to get his money, Tommy. Did you know about the money he kept in the house?"

"Money?" Tommy looked a little dazed. He sobbed in a deep breath and then got control of himself. "Sure, Marshal," he said, then. "I knew he kept his money hidden around the house somewhere. I guess quite a few people did. He never made it any secret that he didn't trust the bank in Dodge."

Dillon shook his head. "It's too bad he felt that way. He might be still alive if he hadn't."

"He used to tell folks that a bank could be robbed and then where would a body's money be?" Chester Good said. "I once argued with him about that, Mr. Dillon. But you couldn't budge Uncle Jeff on that subject. He told me that a robber could always steal his money from the bank, but nobody would ever get it where he had it hid."

"Uncle Jeff was a smart man in a lot of ways," Dillon said. "But like a lot of smart men, there were some things he wasn't very smart about. That was one of them. And, of course, he had the money hidden in the one place that was most obvious—buried under the floor of the kitchen."

"Mebbe he reckoned thieves wouldn't look in the most obvious place," Caleb Weems said. He took the straw from his mouth and broke it between his fingers.

"Is the money gone?" Tommy asked.

Dillon nodded. "Every bit of it, Tommy. You have any idea how much he had?"

Tommy thought about it. Finally he said, "Why, yes, sir. It—well—it was quite a bit. Uncle Jeff was a good farmer and a sharp trader. He knew how to take care of his money too. I mean, that is, how to save. He told me not so long ago that he had at least five thousand dollars saved up."

Caleb Weems whistled.

"Tommy," Dillon said softly, "did your pa know about Uncle Jeff keeping all that money buried under the kitchen floor instead of safe in the bank?"

Tommy blinked away the last of the tears. "Pa?" he said. "Why, I—well, I don't rightly know, Marshal. Maybe he did. I just don't know." Then the direction of the Marshal's questioning began to be apparent to Tommy. "Wait a minute, Marshal. What's Pa got to do with this?"

When Dillon didn't answer right away, Tommy's mouth opened in shocked surprise. He looked at Chester Good and Caleb Weems. Both of them turned their eyes away. Chester was fidgeting uncomfortably.

Tommy turned back to Dillon. "Marshal, you don't think—why, Pa couldn't have anything to do with this. You don't think my father killed Uncle Jeff, do you, Marshal?"

"We don't know, Tommy. We just can't overlook any possibility." Dillon turned toward Chester. "Chester, let me have that tobacco pouch."

Chester stepped forward and handed Dillon a worn-smooth cowhide tobacco pouch. Dillon held the pouch out on the palm of his hand for Tommy to see. He said, "You recognize this, Tommy?"

The tobacco pouch had a crude drawing of an Indian chief's head and the initials J. G. burned into it. Tommy inspected the pouch and then looked up at Marshal Dillon. He shook his head.

"Why, no, Marshal. I don't."

Dillon looked steadily into the boy's eyes. "You're sure of that, Tommy?"

"Yes, sir." He nodded vigorously.

Dillon shook his head wonderingly. "That's kind of strange, Tommy. Those are your father's initials, aren't they? J. G.?"

"Why, yes, sir. I—I suppose they are. What's that got to do with all this?"

"We found this pouch on the floor near Uncle Jeff's body, Tommy. It could have been dropped by the man who killed him. In fact, I don't see any other way it could have got there."

"But my father isn't the only one with the initials J. G., Marshal."

"Around here he is, Tommy."

"But if that was his tobacco pouch, I'd have recognized it, wouldn't I, sir? It couldn't be his. I remember, now— Pa was smoking his pipe last night and he was using another pouch. So, you see, Marshal, that one couldn't be his."

"He could have had two, Tommy." Dillon saw some of

the hope go out of Tommy's face. "But maybe there is some explanation for it being there, son. Maybe your father gave it to Uncle Jeff."

Tommy shook his head dejectedly. "Uh-uh. Uncle Jeff didn't smoke a pipe."

Just then Doc Adams came out of the Foster house, carrying his battered old physician's bag. His lined, mustached face looked more morose than usual. He said, "Nothing more we can do here, Marshal. Guess we'd best—" He broke off, seeing Tommy standing there.

"Mornin', Tommy," Doc Adams said.

"Good morning, Doc." Tommy suddenly thought of something. He gestured toward the house. "My parrot's in there, Marshal. Pluto. I forgot to take him back home with me yesterday. Can I go in and get him?"

Yanking down on the brim of his hat, Dillon said, "I'm afraid that's more bad news, Tommy. The parrot is gone."

"Gone? Pluto gone?"

"There was a struggle in there, Tommy," Chester said. "Looked like old Uncle Jeff put up a good fight for his life, but in the struggle the parrot cage was knocked down and the door sprung open. There are a few green feathers around on the floor but no sign of the bird, so we figured

he must've flown on out the door when the killer left."

Quickly then, seeing the complete misery on Tommy's face at this additional bad news, Marshal Dillon said, "Chances are he didn't go far away, Tommy. When he gets hungry, he'll probably come back. Could be right around here in a tree somewhere. Want to take a quick look?" Dillon gestured toward several big trees around the yard.

As Tommy ran toward the trees, Chester, Doc, and Caleb Weems crowded close around Dillon. Chester said softly, "What do you think, Mr. Dillon? It doesn't look too good for the boy's pa, does it? I mean, finding his tobacco pouch in there and Jan Gant taking off the way he did."

When Dillon didn't answer but continued to stare, eyes narrowed thoughtfully, off into the distance, Chester went on, "What I mean is, Mr. Dillon, he ain't here and the boy said he ain't up to his own place, so he must've run off, don't you think? And only a guilty man would do something like that."

"There's one other possibility, Chester," Dillon said. "Maybe Jan Gant has gone after the killer. Let's hope so, for Tommy's sake. And listen, all of you." He looked around at them. "Don't say too much about how bad it looks for Jan Gant until we're more sure of things—I mean around Tommy. This is rough enough on the boy, without us making it rougher."

"Yes, sir, Mr. Dillon," Chester said. "We won't even talk about it in front of him any more."

"I know you won't, Chester. You'll be going with me."

"Where, Mr. Dillon?"

"We've got to catch up with Jan Gant, wherever he's gone, and have a talk with him." Dillon turned to Doc. "Doc, you and Caleb Weems hitch up Uncle Jeff's buckboard and tote his body into Dodge, to the undertaker. Weems can drive the buckboard. Doc, you take the boy on into town with you. Sort of keep an eye on him for me until we get back."

Doc Adams snorted, blowing out his mustache. "Oh, that's just fine, Marshal. You really pick the nice, easy jobs for me, don't you? What am I supposed to do with a boy whose father has just been released from prison on a murder charge and now is the number one suspect in the slaying and robbery of an old man who was just about his best friend? What am I supposed to talk to him about?"

Dillon smiled grimly. "You'll figure it out, Doc, when the time comes. A good doctor knows the right things to say to people who are sick in spirit as well as those who're sick in body. Isn't that so, Doc?"

"I know, but dad-drat it, Matt, couldn't somebody else—"

Before he could finish, Dillon said, "Doc, you wouldn't be tryin' to squirm out of a duty you know darned well is really yours, would you? You know Chester and I have to go after his father, don't you?"

Doc Adams scuffed dirt with his shoe. "Oh, all right then." He glowered up at Matt Dillon. "Go on. What are you two standing around jawin' for? Get about your business."

Dillon turned toward the hitching rail. "Come on, Chester."

As he mounted, Dillon nodded toward Tommy Gant, who was sitting under a tree, his arms folded across his upthrust knees, his face buried in his arms. Dillon said, "Look at him, Chester. It's a rotten shame. It's really beginning to hit the boy now."

"You mean about his father, Mr. Dillon?"

"No. I don't think he's really seriously considered that his father could be the killer yet. What's hitting him now is the realization that Uncle Jeff Foster is dead. Actually it's probably worse for Tommy than if it was his real father that had been killed. You could tell that boy loved old Uncle Jeff something special. He's going to take it really hard, the more it sinks in."

"Good gracious, Mr. Dillon, then you can imagine how it'll be for poor Tommy, if it turns out that it *was* his father who killed Uncle Jeff."

"Yeah," Dillon said.

After a moment, then, Chester said, "But it'll have to be somebody else, don't you think? I mean, a man couldn't rob and kill an old neighbor and friend who's taken such good care of his family, helped 'em out so much while he was away and all. Could he, Mr. Dillon?"

"I hope not, Chester. We've got one hope against that."

"What's that?"

"A man named Huggins. He was in the penitentiary with Jan Gant. And Huggins was in Dodge yesterday and last night. What I'm hoping, Chester, is that Huggins is the killer and that maybe Gant saw him escaping and went after him. If it wasn't Huggins, it doesn't leave anybody much but Gant, so far as I can see, at this point."

Chester thought about that. Finally he said, "But this man—Huggins, is it? He's a stranger, Mr. Dillon. How would he know Uncle Jeff kept a lot of money buried under the floor of his kitchen?"

"There are ways he could have found that out, Chester. In prison there isn't much for men to do to pass the time, but talk. Gant might have mentioned something about Uncle Jeff and his mistrust of banks, not even thinking that later some convict might remember that when he got out and go after the money."

"I see," Chester said. Then he blurted, "There's one other possibility, too, then, Mr. Dillon."

"I know. That Huggins and Gant were in it together. I've been trying not to think about that, Chester."

They rode on a little faster.

4   *Manhunt*

Knowing that Jan Gant would not have headed back toward Dodge, Marshal Dillon and Chester figured that he had probably struck out for the northern part of the state. After first making a thorough search around the Gant homestead to make sure the missing man wasn't hiding somewhere there, they picked up his trail, a few hundred yards from the house, leading across country.

Several times during the next hour or so, as they headed into wild and rolling prairie land, Dillon and Chester lost precious time when the trail became lost or blurred.

Once Chester said, "Gosh, Mr. Dillon, we'll never catch up to him at this rate. No tellin' how much of a head start he has on us, and we get farther behind every blessed time the trail fades out. You reckon we'll ever catch him?"

"I don't know, Chester. I wouldn't admit it to anybody

else but you, but every once in a while I'm hoping we won't catch up with Gant, if he's the guilty one."

"I know it, Mr. Dillon. I've been thinkin' the same thing myself. Of course, that ain't right, us bein' lawmen and all, is it? But then, if it turned out that way, poor Tommy at least wouldn't ever know for sure that it was his pa."

"Well, that could be even worse in some ways."

"How do you figure it?"

"Sometimes *not* knowing a thing—thinking one way one minute and another the next—can be even worse."

The trail they were following became quite clear then and for a few miles they were able to make better time. Conversation between them faded out. Then, about an hour later, Marshal Dillon reined in and pointed toward the sky some distance ahead and off to the left. Several buzzards were wheeling and dipping in slow, purposeful circles.

"Something dead over there, Mr. Dillon. Probably just an animal of some kind."

"Most likely. But we'd better check."

They rode on, still following the marks of Jan Gant's horse's hoofprints, until they suddenly veered left in the direction of the place over which the buzzards were hovering. A few moments later they saw the thing that had attracted the death-birds. A horse was sprawled on its side.

"That's Gant's mount," Dillon said. He looked around, then back at the dead horse. "Shot in the head. See the way his foreleg's twisted, Chester. Looks as though he stepped in a gopher hole and broke it and Gant had to do away with him."

"That's it, all right, Mr. Dillon. Tough luck for Gant, but a good deal for us. He can't make very fast time on foot. We've got a good chance to catch up with him, now."

"Yeah. Let's get going, Chester."

They rode on. About an hour later, following the trail Jan Gant had left, moving on foot, Marshal Dillon reached toward Chester. Almost whispering, he said, "Hold it a minute. I've got a feeling we've reached the end of the trail. Almost, anyhow."

"How do you mean, a feelin', Mr. Dillon?"

"I don't know how to explain it exactly, but when you've tracked down as many men as I have, you get a sort of extra sense that seems to tell you when you're near your quarry. I've got that feeling right now. It's sort of a feeling as though somebody is watching you."

Shielding his eyes against the sun, Dillon looked carefully around the surrounding country. After a moment he said, "It may very well be that we *are* being watched, right this minute."

"You think Gant is hiding around here, someplace, waiting for us to ride past?"

Off to the right there was a sharp rise of ground and on top of it a formation of large glacial boulders.

"You see those rocks up there, Chester? If a man was going to hole up somewhere and try to fight off capture, that would be a mighty good spot."

"Sure would be, Mr. Dillon. You think Gant heard us and decided to pick that place to either hide and let us ride by—or to fight it out, if we spotted him."

"Yes. Let's ride up that way and see. But ride slowly, Chester. Keep your eyes on those rocks and at the first sign of a rifle flash in the sun, hit the ground fast and head for the nearest thicket. If Gant did kill Uncle Jeff, he's not going to think twice about getting us too."

"Don't worry about me, Mr. Dillon. If Gant shoots I'll hit that ground so hard I'll likely go right through to China."

"When he shoots, it might be too late, Chester. You can't move faster than a bullet."

Cautiously they moved across a flat, sparsely grassed field, toward the beginning of the rise of ground topped by the big boulders. They hadn't gone more than a hundred yards when a bullet whistled over their heads.

"Down, Chester!" Dillon ordered, slipping swiftly from the saddle himself and sprawling into the grass. "Hit for those thickets over there!"

Between two rocks, up there on the hill, he saw the momentary glint of sun on the barrel of a rifle. At the same time, Jan Gant called to them, "Don't come any closer. The next time I won't shoot over your heads, Marshal."

The two lawmen slithered through the thin grass, toward the nearest and largest clump of shrubbery. Crouched down behind it, Dillon took off his hat and sleeved sweat and dirt from his face.

"That was too close for comfort," Chester said. "And he could have killed one of us, right off."

"I know. That's what he'll try to do next time. Gant isn't the type to make statements like that unless he means it. We're in a tight spot, Chester. I wish I knew what's best to do."

"One thing's sure. We can't rush him, up on that hill. There isn't enough protection. We wouldn't have a chance."

Dillon nodded in silent agreement.

"How about one of us circling around on the other side of that hill, Mr. Dillon?"

"I've thought about that. So has Gant, I'm sure. He'll be looking for that. And anyone trying to get at him from the other side would have that bright sun full in his eyes. He'd be helplessly blinded."

"He sure picked a good spot then, didn't he?"

"It couldn't be better. But let's see if we can talk him out of it."

Dillon cupped his hands about his mouth and shouted, "Jan Gant! Can you hear me?"

There was a moment's delay and then an answering shout: "I hear you all right, Marshal, but you can save your breath. You're not talking me into anything."

"Gant!" Dillon answered. "I've got to take you back to Dodge, whether you killed Uncle Jeff or not. If you're innocent and can prove it, there won't be anything to it. If you're guilty, you'll have to stand trial. Now come down from there, Gant, with your hands over your head."

"I didn't kill Foster but I can't prove it, Marshal, so you're out of luck. I'm not turning myself in."

"That isn't the way a really innocent man would act,

Gant. If you're innocent, you have nothing to fear. The law's on your side."

There was silence for a moment. Then Gant shouted, "Don't make me laugh, Marshal. What chance would I have at a trial—an ex-convict? Everybody will think I did it. Whether I really did or not won't matter."

"That's not so, Gant," Dillon answered. "If you didn't do it, we'll get the one who did. Look, Gant, let's be sensible. Come down here and talk it over."

"Not a chance, Marshal. You're not taking me back to Dodge. Not alive, anyhow."

"Then it'll have to be the other way, Gant. You can't defy the law and get away with it."

"Mr. Dillon," Chester said, "mention Tommy. Maybe that'll put some sense in his stubborn head."

"That's a good idea, Chester. Thanks." Dillon raised his voice again, shouting between cupped hands, "What about your boy, Gant? How do you think it'll be for him to have his father shot down as a fugitive from the law?"

"Not any worse, Marshal, than it will be to have a court of prejudiced people convict me as a killer. . . . Listen, Marshal, all this talk is senseless. You aren't takin' me in and that's final. Now both of you get out from behind that shrubbery, head for your horses, and ride back to Dodge without me."

"If we don't . . . ?"

"Then you give me no choice, Marshal. I'll have to pepper those bushes with lead until I kill one or both of you, because I've got to keep goin'. I've got to get away."

"How far can you get, Gant, without a mount?"

"I'll get another horse up the line, somewhere. Marshal, now I'm givin' you until the count of three and then I'm going to start shooting, if you and Chester don't come out of there with your hands up and head for your horses."

"What are we goin' to do, Mr. Dillon? He means business," Chester said.

"I don't know, Chester. I'd been hoping we were wrong and that Gant wasn't guilty, but the way he's acting doesn't make it look very good for him. I guess if it has to be him or us, that's the way it's got to be."

Then he shouted, "Go ahead and start shooting, Gant. We'll give it right back to you, shot for shot. You're shielded by those rocks but a bullet can ricochet off one of them and still get you. And we've got two guns against your one."

The answer to that was the keening whine of a bullet, and a slashing noise as it cut through the shrubbery a few feet away from where Dillon and Chester crouched. Both of them hunched their heads down into their shoulders. Chester made a wincing face at Dillon.

"All right," Dillon said. "He's called the cards. We've got to give it back to him."

They both took aim with their six-guns and fired up toward the rocks. When the echo of the shots died away, Chester said, "At this long range, our forty-fours aren't much of a match for that rifle of Gant's."

"That's all right, Chester. We don't want to kill him if we can help it, anyhow. But with all those rocks around him, for the slugs to ricochet from, lead will be buzzing around Gant's head enough to make him plenty nervous. Let's give him another round. Empty your gun this time."

They did that. Little spurts of dust flew from the rocks up on top of the rise. There was the distant whining sound of the bullets ricocheting up there. Then there was no sound at all, as Dillon and Chester reloaded.

"Awful quiet up there, Mr. Dillon," Chester said. "You think we got him with a lucky shot?"

Before Dillon could reply, another shot sounded from Jan Gant's rock fortress. A thick twig snapped near Chester's head.

"There's your answer, Chester," Dillon said.

From up on the hill, Gant shouted, "Why don't you leave me alone, Marshal. I don't want to have to kill either of you. Don't make me do it, Marshal, you hear?"

"That's the only way you'll get rid of us," Dillon hollered back. "You aren't even making sense, Gant. You kill one of us and you *know* you'll hang. Give yourself up and you'll at least have a fighting chance."

"All right, if that's the way you want it, Marshal," Gant answered. "They'll hang me anyhow, if I go back to Dodge with you."

"What makes you so certain of that, Gant? An innocent man can usually prove his innocence."

"That's the trouble. I can't, Marshal. All I have is my own word. Who in Dodge will pay any attention to that? I tell you, I'm not letting you take me in and that's final."

The echo of Gant's voice had hardly faded when there was another sound from behind Dillon and Chester. The rataplan of flying hoofs startled them both. Dillon turned his head and saw a rider bearing down on them at full gallop. Then a voice shouted, "Marshal Dillon, it's me— Tommy Gant!"

"Great day in the mornin', Mr. Dillon!" Chester

exclaimed. "What's that kid doin' way out here?"

"I don't know, Chester, but we'll soon find out." Dillon shouted toward the rocky hilltop. "Gant, hold your fire! Your son, Tommy, is riding this way. You hear me?"

"I hear you, Marshal. But don't think that's going to make any difference. It won't. Nothing's going to change my mind about going back with you."

"Maybe not," Dillon told Chester. "But he sure didn't sound too confident about that. Maybe this is a piece of good luck for us." He stood up and waved toward Tommy Gant, who rode close to them and then dismounted.

Tommy Gant's face was streaked with dust and sweat. He looked pale and haggard; his eyes seemed too large for his thin face.

"Marshal," Tommy said, "I ran out on Doc Adams. I'm sorry, Marshal, but I had to do it."

"Why, Tommy?"

"Well, I knew you were going after my father and I— I know how stubborn Pa can be. I was afraid that if you caught up with him, he'd fight and you might have to kill him. I was hoping I could stop that somehow."

"I see. How did you get away from Doc? He's going to be plenty mad at you about that, Tommy."

"I can't help it, sir. It was easy to escape. You see," Tommy grinned ruefully, "Doc doesn't ride so good."

Dillon fought back a small smile. "I think I know what you mean."

"Huh!" Chester grunted. "Me too. Doc sits a horse like a Hottentot ridin' a sway-backed mule."

"Marshal," Tommy Gant said, "I won't believe Pa killed and robbed Uncle Jeff Foster, unless I hear it from him."

"Now, hold on, Tommy. You don't think he'll come right out and admit he did it, if he did, do you, boy?"

Tommy shook his head. "Uh-uh. Probably not. But if I ask him point-blank and he *did* do it, he won't deny it."

"What makes you so sure of that, Tommy? Maybe he would lie under those circumstances, just to save you the pain of knowing the truth."

"No, he wouldn't, Marshal. Back before he went away, when I was still a little kid, Pa and I made a solemn pact never to lie to each other. Not about anything, Marshal. We made the pact under oath. Maybe you think that won't mean anything to Pa at a time like this, but I know it will, Marshal."

Dillon and Chester looked at each other. Then Dillon put his hand on Tommy's shoulder. "Tommy, let me try to explain something to you. What you believe about your pa—or what I believe, even—doesn't count much in a matter like this. Even if your pa is innocent, there's still quite a bit of evidence against him. It's not for us—not even for me—to decide what the truth is. But if he is innocent, Tommy, we'll do everything we can to prove that. We'll get the real killer. The point is, I've still got to bring your pa in. Do you understand that?"

"I guess so." Tommy nodded. "Why don't you tell him that?"

"We already did. He doesn't believe it, Tommy. He's afraid he's going to be blamed for the killing no matter what, because of that threat against Uncle Jeff's life he made at the trial, I suppose. And because he's a man who just got out of prison."

"If I could talk with him, Marshal, maybe I could make him see the thing right, get him to give himself up."

For a long moment Marshal Dillon stared thoughtfully at Tommy Gant. Then he said, "Maybe you could at that."

"Wait a minute, Mr. Dillon," Chester cut in. "Suppose he holds the boy hostage—you know, uses him as a shield or something? We couldn't shoot, then. If he's desperate enough, he might well do that, Mr. Dillon."

Dillon thought about it. "Yeah." He turned to Tommy. "What about that?"

Eagerly the boy said, "I'll see that doesn't happen, Marshal. I won't get close enough for him to grab me, unless he promises not to."

Dillon looked at Chester. "What do you think?"

"Well, we'll be takin' a chance. But it might be a good bet, Mr. Dillon."

"There's only one thing, Marshal," Tommy said, then. "Maybe I can get Pa to come back with me if he's innocent. If he really did kill Uncle Jeff, I probably won't be able to."

"How come, Tommy?"

"Well, I—I'm goin' to have to kind of play a trick on Pa, to get him to give himself up. If he tells me he didn't kill Uncle Jeff, then I'll tell him that I won't believe him unless he turns himself over to you. You see, Marshal? If he wants me to believe him, he'll have to do that. . . . But that's why, if he is the killer, I won't be able to bring him back."

For a few moments, Marshal Dillon didn't say anything. Then, finally, he slapped Tommy on the back. "All right, son. I don't see where we have anything to lose. Go to it. And I promise you that if you bring your pa back to me,

I'll do everything I can to help him." He raised his right hand. "That's an oath, too, Tommy."

Tommy nodded solemnly and walked away, headed toward the foot of the hill. As soon as Jan Gant saw that his son was coming toward him, he shouted, "No, Tommy! You can't come up here. Go on back!"

Tommy kept walking. "I've got to talk to you, Pa," he shouted. "I'm coming up there. I've got to."

"No, Tommy! You stay down there. Go back with the Marshal, you hear me? That's an order, Tommy."

"I'm sorry, sir. I—I can't do that. I've got to talk with you privately. I don't like to disobey, but this time I have to."

Several more times, with increasing anger and some panic in his voice, Jan Gant tried to stop his son. It didn't do any good. Tommy kept climbing up the hill.

Below, Chester and Marshal Dillon watched anxiously. "I'm tellin' you, Mr. Dillon, that boy's got spunk," Chester said, shaking his head admiringly.

"Sure has, Chester. I hope for his sake, maybe even more than for Gant's, that his father wasn't the one. That boy's been through enough as it is."

Then they both remained silent, shifting nervously about

as they waited to see what would happen. Tommy Gant was up there in the rock formation now. Dillon could see him, leaning against one of the rocks, talking to the man hiding behind it.

A few minutes later, Chester and the Marshal saw the boy turn slowly around and walk away. Alone. Dillon looked at Chester and both of them let out sighs of disappointment.

"Looks as though it didn't work, Mr. Dillon. I was hardly darin' to hope that it might."

"Well, we tried anyhow, Chester. I wonder what it means—the boy coming back alone—that Gant *was* the killer and, like Tommy said, just couldn't lie to him about it, or—"

Dillon broke off the sentence as suddenly they saw Jan Gant's big awkward figure move out from behind a rock. They saw him reach toward Tommy. They heard him shout, "Wait, Tommy! You win. I'll go with you."

Marshal Dillon and Chester looked at each other again. They both grinned. But the grin swiftly slipped from Dillon's face. He wiped his hands up and down the sides of his Levi's.

"All I hope now, Chester, is that Gant can *help* us prove

his innocence in some way. If he can't, we might have a hopeless job on our hands."

Closer now, Tommy Gant, walking beside his father, called out, "It's all right, Marshal. You can take your hands away from your guns. Pa promised me he wouldn't make any more trouble."

"All right, Tommy," Dillon told him.

Gant walked up to Dillon and handed over his rifle. "I'm afraid this is the biggest mistake I ever made in my life, Marshal," he said, scowling darkly. "I haven't got a chance and you know that too. But at least, now, my son knows I didn't kill Uncle Jeff."

5   *Buried Loot*

Marshal Dillon took Gant's rifle and handed it to Chester. At the same time he said, "Gant, if you're innocent, you haven't got too much to worry about. You made a big mistake, though, running away. Why did you run?"

Gant shrugged his great, rawboned shoulders. "I thought it would be better, Marshal. Not for me, understand. But for my wife and boy."

"How could you figure that?"

Gant wiped dust and perspiration from under his deeply sunken, haunted-looking eyes. "Well, as soon as I saw poor old Uncle Jeff had been robbed and killed, I knew I'd be suspected. You know how in court after I was convicted on the Logart killing, I shouted that when I got out of prison I'd kill both Mike Galloway and Uncle Jeff, too, for testifying against me. Well, the first night I'm back home, sure enough, Uncle Jeff gets killed. Who would folks think of first as the killer?"

"You'd probably be asked some questions, all right," Dillon agreed. "That wouldn't mean you couldn't clear yourself."

"Marshal," Gant said tiredly, "Uncle Jeff Foster was a well-liked man in Dodge. Feelings are going to run high when folks hear about his murder. Folks in Dodge just aren't going to be thinking too clearly, Marshal, or be much inclined to wait around for an investigation. The finger of guilt just naturally points at me and that's all folks would need. I figured I didn't have a chance, Marshal. It just looked to me as though it wasn't meant for me to come back and have an even chance at starting over. It was too much for me to face. I decided that Tommy and the missus would be better off if I just wasn't around. I thought that maybe later, if the real killer was ever caught, then it would be safe for me to come back."

"I see. Suppose you tell me what you *do* know about Uncle Jeff's death, Gant."

His shoulders sagging dejectedly, Gant said, "The more I think about it, Marshal, the worse it does look for me. But since I'm facing up to things, I might as well tell the whole truth, no matter how bad it looks."

Dillon nodded. Tommy and Chester stood by, their eyes on Gant, their ears straining to catch every word of his low-toned voice.

Then Gant reached inside his shirt and took out a sheaf of greenbacks. He handed them to Marshal Dillon.

"This money's Uncle Jeff Foster's, Marshal," he said. "Two hundred dollars of it. You'd have searched me and found it when we got to the jail, anyhow."

"How do you happen to have it, Gant?"

"Uncle Jeff loaned it to me. Last night, after Tommy went to sleep, I couldn't seem to get used to being home in my own bed again. My mind was filled with a million thoughts. I got up and went outside. I saw that Uncle Jeff's lights were still on. He sometimes sits up late reading, you know."

"I know."

"Well, I went down there and we talked about a lot of things, including a saw I wanted to borrow from him the next day. To make it short, Uncle Jeff realized that things were going to be pretty tight with us for a while—having to pay Doc Adams' bill, buying new supplies of feed and stuff, with people maybe not wanting to give a jailbird much

credit. So he offered to lend me that money. I—well—bad as I needed it, I wasn't going to take it, at first. But Uncle Jeff insisted."

"Uh-huh." Marshal Dillon rolled out his lower lip thoughtfully. "Where did Uncle Jeff have this money?"

"He had it hidden, Marshal. He dug under the floor of the kitchen and pulled out a metal box where he kept his savings. He showed me how much he had in there so that I wouldn't feel too bad about what he was loaning me, so I could see he had plenty to spare."

"How much would you say he had in that box, Gant?"

Gant paused a moment. Finally he said, "Be hard to estimate, Marshal. I didn't count it, of course. I'd say maybe several thousand dollars, at least."

"What did Uncle Jeff do with the box full of money, after he gave you the two hundred?"

"He buried the box again, Marshal."

"Then what happened?"

"Why, we just talked awhile longer and then I went on home and went to bed."

"In other words, Foster was alive at that time?"

"Yes. Then early this morning—it wasn't quite dawn, even—I woke up. Prison gives you the habit of waking early, Marshal," Gant said with a wry grin. "Tommy still wasn't awake, so I thought I'd go down to Uncle Jeff's again. The night before, he'd agreed to let me borrow his buckboard to go get the missus this morning. I figured I'd go down and hitch it up and be all ready to travel when Tommy woke up."

Gant paused again and put his big hand up over his eyes. For a moment he swayed dizzily. Dillon said sharply, "You all right, Gant?"

The other man dropped his hand from over his eyes. He shook his head. "Yeah, I'm all right now, Marshal. Seein' poor old Uncle Jeff the way he was, when I went down there this morning, was a bad shock. For a moment, I could see it all over again and it got me."

"He was dead when you got there this morning?"

Gant nodded without speaking.

"It's too bad you didn't ride into town, right then, to notify me," Dillon said.

"I saw the hole where his money had been dug up, Marshal. I knew I didn't have the money but that didn't prove anything. They'd say I could have buried it some-where, hidden it. I didn't know what to do, Marshal. Then it came to me quite clear that I was going to be blamed for it. The more I thought about it the worse it looked for me. When I got back to the house and found Tommy still sleeping, I knew I had to run for it."

"Well," Dillon said, "let's all saddle up and head back for Dodge. We can talk about it some more on the way."

A few minutes later, with Tommy and his father both riding Tommy's horse, they were moving back toward Dodge City.

As they rode, Marshal Dillon said, "Gant, you own a tobacco pouch with the picture of an Indian chief and your initials burned into it?"

Jan Gant's drawn face registered surprise. "Why, yes, Marshal. That is, I *did*."

"What does that mean?"

"I worked in the leatherwork shop at the pen, for a time," Gant said. "I made that tobacco pouch for myself while I was there. How do you know about it, Marshal? When I was packing to leave my cell, in the excitement I must've misplaced the pouch or something. Anyhow, I didn't have it when I got home. I must've left it behind in the cell. I suppose it fell under the bunk or something. How do you know about that pouch, Marshal?"

"We found it under Uncle Jeff Foster's body, Gant."

Dillon held out the pouch for Gant to see. "Can you prove you left it at the prison, Gant?"

Gant looked ill. "It was—under Uncle Jeff's body? That really ties the murder to me, doesn't it?"

"It certainly doesn't make things look any better. But you didn't answer my question."

Gant pounded his right fist into the palm of his left hand. He turned bleak eyes toward Matt Dillon. "Huggins," he said. "He must be the killer, Marshal—Vince Huggins, the man you saw talking to me in front of the Long Branch yesterday."

"What's he got to do with it?"

"Huggins was my cell mate, Marshal. I never liked the man—we never did get along—but you don't have a choice of cell mates. Anyhow, Huggins was due to get out the day after I did. He must've found that tobacco pouch."

"He didn't come out to your place, after I left you yesterday?" Dillon asked.

"No, Marshal." Gant shook his head. "Ask Tommy."

"He could have come out later, after Tommy was asleep."

"But he didn't."

"That's strange. He told Mike Galloway—and some others—that he was going to stay at your place."

"He wanted to, Marshal. That's what we were arguing about in front of the Long Branch yesterday afternoon. But I told him he couldn't. When he still insisted, I told him I'd throw him off the place if he ever showed up out there. He knew I meant it."

"How would Huggins know about Uncle Jeff's hidden money, Gant?"

Gant looked puzzled. "I don't know. But he could have heard about it somewhere."

"You ever mention Uncle Jeff—and his savings when you were in prison?"

"I might have. I'm not sure. We all talked about our family, our friends and neighbors, a lot. That is, those of us who had any. I just don't remember, Marshal."

"Well, if Huggins is the killer, we'll find it out," Dillon said. "He's had too much of a head start for us ever to catch him now. But if I get some kind of solid proof against him, I'll get out a Wanted dodger."

Gant looked surprised. "Proof, Marshal? What more proof could you want than that tobacco pouch of mine?"

When Dillon didn't answer, Gant said, "I see. That isn't really proof against *him,* is it? You've only got my word that the pouch was in his possession."

"That doesn't mean I'm counting Huggins out, though, Gant. And if he's our man, we'll find some other evidence. Somebody will have seen him out that way or something. Every killer makes a slip-up of some kind."

They rode on in silence for a while, until Jan Gant said, "Tommy, you haven't said much since I gave myself up. Do you—well—still believe me, Tommy?"

"You gave me your word, sir, didn't you?" Tommy answered.

"Suppose they never catch up with Huggins, or whoever is the real killer, Tommy? And things look worse and worse for me?"

"That won't happen," Tommy blurted desperately. "The real killer will be found if I have to go out and hunt him down myself. Marshal Dillon, you believe in my pa, don't you?"

"It's not my job to make such a judgment, Tommy. But I will say this—I go along with the law, which says that a man is innocent until proven guilty. Does that help?"

"Yes, sir. But I don't mean officially. I mean in your own mind—in your own heart, Marshal?"

"Tommy, it's hard for me to answer a question like that, in the face of the only evidence we have. Let me just say that I hope your pa is an innocent man and that he hasn't lied to you."

"Chester," Tommy said, "how about you?"

With a hangdog, uncomfortable look, Chester said, "Uh—what was that, Tommy? I—ah—you see, I reckon I wasn't listening too closely." The way he said it, it was obvious that he was lying.

"I asked you about my father," Tommy persisted. "Do you believe in him?"

Chester stammered and stuttered. Finally he said, unconvincingly, "Well, let's just say I go along with the Marshal's sentiments, Tommy. Yeah, let's just say I agree with Mr. Dillon, all the way."

"That's passing the buck neatly, Chester," Dillon said. "Tommy, I'm sure Chester hopes, just as I do, that we'll be able to clear your father—and soon."

"Yes, sir," Chester said. "That's exactly what I meant."

"And you will work on tryin' to find out who really did do it, then, Marshal?" Tommy persisted.

"You can count on that, Tommy. I'll follow down any slightest lead, no matter how thin it might seem."

"Thanks, Marshal," Tommy said. "I feel better now."

About an hour later they passed the Gant place. Tommy

kept his eyes averted. So did his father. Dillon and Chester made no comment. Both were aware that this was a trying moment for Tommy and his father. They urged their mounts on a little faster until the well-built but weather-beaten house and outbuildings were no longer in sight.

Then, as the trail led them past the boundary marker that divided the Foster and Gant homestead properties, a flash of green darted from a grove of trees off to the right. There was the whirring of heavy wings and a scolding, chattering sound as Tommy's now ruffled and slightly battered-looking parrot flew around the group and then fluttered back toward the trees.

"Pluto!" Tommy cried. "It's my parrot. He's all right.... Pa, ride over to that grove. I've got to get him."

"Sure looked like he recognized you, Tommy," Marshal Dillon said, smiling.

"And plenty glad to see him too," Chester added. "Evidently he's decided he doesn't take too much to having his freedom."

The four of them turned toward the grove. As Tommy dismounted, the parrot, perched on a low limb, suddenly swooped toward the ground and picked something up in his beak. He then flew toward Tommy and settled down on the boy's outstretched arm. His hooded eyes blinking wisely, the parrot now took the large silver coin he held in his beak and flipped it to one side. Caught by surprise, Tommy missed catching the coin and it fell to the ground.

"Filthy lucre!" the parrot screamed. "The root of all evil! Filthy lucre!"

Marshal Dillon quickly picked up the coin the parrot had flung away. He flipped it and caught it in his palm.

"Now where did he find this?" Dillon wondered aloud. "A cartwheel. A silver dollar. . . . He picked it up from the ground over there. Chester, let's go have a look. Maybe there's more there."

While Tommy smoothed down the parrot's ruffled feathers and talked comfortingly to him, Dillon and Chester walked slowly around the grove of trees, their eyes turned to the ground.

"You thinkin' the same thing I am, Mr. Dillon?" Chester asked.

"Could be, Chester. If you're thinking that maybe that bird followed whoever killed Uncle Jeff and that while he was burying the loot, he dropped some coins. It's a good hunch, anyhow. Can't lose anything by looking around."

They searched the ground in the grove for several minutes

without success. They were just about to give up when
Dillon pointed to a large, flat rock near a clump of thorn-
bush.

"Chester, look at that flat rock. And that slight indenta-
tion in the grass around it. Would you say that rock might
have been moved recently?"

Chester limped up beside Dillon and stood with him,
looking down at the rock. "I sure would, Mr. Dillon," he
said. "In fact, I'd bet on it."

"Well, let's move it again and take a look underneath."

They bent together, took hold of the rock, and flipped
it over. Dillon said, "Better get that small spade you carry
in your saddle pack, Chester."

While Chester was gone to do that, Marshal Dillon
looked at Jan Gant, who had walked over with Tommy
to watch. "Gant," Dillon said, "whose property is this,
right here?"

Gant looked around toward the boundary marker
nearby. "Why, mine, Marshal," he answered.

"That's what I was afraid of."

"Afraid of? What do you mean?"

"Well, sir, if we find Uncle Jeff Foster's money box
buried here, the fact that it was found on your property

isn't going to make things look any better for you."

Almost angrily, Jan Gant said, "Look, Marshal, if I'd killed Foster and buried that money, I wouldn't hide it on my own property, would I? And if I was the one, would I stand here while you dug it up? Wouldn't I figure your finding the money really cooked my goose and try to get away? Several times while you and Chester were looking around in this grove, I could have gotten away."

"That's right," Dillon admitted. "I can see it that way, all right. But with the other evidence against you, maybe folks will figure it differently. . . . Here comes Chester with the spade. Maybe the money isn't even buried here. We'll see."

It was. Chester hadn't dug down more than a foot when the spade scraped against the top of the metal box. A few minutes later, Dillon reached into the hole and pulled out the old-fashioned strongbox. He brushed dirt from it and opened the latch. Inside, wrapped in oiled paper to keep out moisture, was a packet of money. In the bottom of the box, lying loose, were about twenty or thirty silver dollars.

Quickly, Dillon unwrapped the money packet and riffled through the greenbacks, counting rapidly as he did so. His eyebrows raised in surprise, he turned to the others.

"Why, there's only about five hundred dollars here. Maybe even a little less, at a completely accurate count."

"Even counting the cartwheels, Mr. Dillon?"

"Even counting them, Chester." The Marshal turned to Jan Gant. "Are you sure there was as much as you thought in this box, when you saw it last night at Uncle Jeff's?"

Jan Gant's rugged face showed as much surprise as the others. "Yes, sir. I'm sure, all right. In fact, there were several more packets of money like that, some of them with the bills in larger denominations."

"You couldn't possibly have been mistaken?"

"No, sir."

"Good gracious, Mr. Dillon," Chester said, frowning in bewilderment. "Why would the killer bury only part of the money? And that's what he's done, if Mr. Gant knows what he's talkin' about."

Dillon looked long and steadily at Jan Gant, his keen eyes searching to see if the other man was telling the whole truth.

Finally Dillon said, "It sure looks that way, Chester."

"But why would he do that, sir?" Tommy demanded.

"That's what I've been wondering, Tommy," Dillon said. "And maybe I'm beginning to get an answer. It's only a theory and even if it's true, it'll be hard to prove. But it makes sense to me."

"What is it, Marshal?" Tommy asked excitedly.

Dillon turned his attention back to Jan Gant. He said, "Gant, how does this sound to you? First off, was Vince Huggins a drinking man?"

"Well," Gant said hesitantly, "I—why, I'm not sure, Marshal. Seems to me I did smell liquor on his breath yesterday when I was talking to him. But then, he may just have had one drink or so. Why?"

"It doesn't really matter," Dillon said. "I was just trying to find an excuse for a man doing something as rotten as what I had in mind. But maybe Huggins was vicious enough even to do it sober. Listen, Gant, suppose late last night Huggins rode out this way, figuring to try to talk you into letting him spend the night at your place—or at least to get a meal and feed for his horse, if he was short of cash."

"Yes," Gant said, "he might have done that. He was a pretty stubborn man. Even though I'd told him I'd throw him off the place, he might have figured I'd weaken and let him stay for the night. Be pretty hard to send anyone on their way late at night like that, if they were tired and hungry. I might even have let him sleep in the stable or someplace, if he promised to clear out early in the morning before Tommy woke up."

"All right," Dillon said, his eyes narrowing. "Then suppose this Huggins spotted you going into Uncle Jeff's house, last night, to talk with him. Let's say he watched what went on through a window, saw Uncle Jeff dig up the money box and give you that loan. Let's say he got a pretty good idea that there was a lot more cash in that box. Wouldn't that tempt a man like Huggins, Gant?"

Jan Gant's rough-hewn face began to show understanding. "I—well I reckon it would, Marshal."

"What was Huggins serving time in the pen for, Gant?"

"A holdup, Marshal. He robbed a stage station and got caught."

"All right. So Huggins waits for you to leave, Gant, and then he goes in and sticks up Uncle Jeff. But the old fellow gave him a fight, tried to grab his gun or something, and Huggins hit him too hard and killed him."

"Yeah," Chester said enthusiastically. "Yeah, that could have happened, Mr. Dillon."

"Then he got scared and tried to make it look like my pa had done it," Tommy put in. "He left that tobacco pouch there with Pa's initials on it, and buried part of the money on our place. Maybe he even *brought* Pluto up here, figuring the bird would stay around and attract our attention to this spot."

"That's right, Mr. Dillon," Chester said. "He certainly didn't make much of an effort to hide that money where nobody would find it. Anybody looking around here would have been bound to spot that rock having been moved. Looks to me like we've got the whole thing figured out."

"Uh-huh," Dillon said, wrapping the money back up in the oiled paper and putting it back into the box. This he then handed to Chester. "Put this in your saddlebag, Chester. We'll need it as evidence. . . . There's only one thing wrong."

"What's that, Marshal?" Tommy asked, his eyes shining hopefully, still.

"We'll have to bring Huggins back from wherever he's run off to, to prove it all."

"Oh!" Tommy said, and his shoulders sagged dejectedly.

Dillon put his arm around the boy's shoulder. "Cheer up, Tommy. It'll probably take some time, but we'll get him. I'll wire pickup orders to all the towns north of here. Huggins probably won't be too careful about showing himself and spending some of that money. He'll figure he's safe after making it look so bad for your pa."

After a pause, Dillon added, "In the meantime, Mr. Gant, I'm afraid I'll still have to keep you in custody, in the face of the actual evidence I have—and because Huggins figures, right now, in theory only. But if we're right —and you really are in the clear, have played straight with me, Gant—it'll be merely a technicality, until we've got Huggins."

Jan Gant sighed. He smiled grimly. "I understand, Marshal. At last now I have some hope. Eh, Tommy?" He reached out and lightly punched Tommy's arm, his deeply sunken eyes softened and alight with affection.

"Yes, sir!" Tommy said, as they started back toward the horses.

Pluto the parrot was still perched comfortably on Tommy's extended arm. As Tommy prepared to mount behind his father, Pluto fluttered to Tommy's shoulder. He stayed there, blinking contentedly.

6   *The Angry Town*

Earlier that day, Caleb Weems had driven into Dodge with Uncle Jeff Foster's body, after which he had lost no time in spreading the news.

Soon the bar at the Long Branch was jammed with shocked townsmen, some of whom had done business with Uncle Jeff for years and were personal friends as well.

In the center of the crowd was Caleb Weems, his toothless mouth pursed importantly, his wrinkled face glowing. His shrewd little eyes gleamed delightedly at the attention being awarded him as he was called on again and again to tell his story of discovering the murder.

For years old Caleb Weems had been a nobody, a lazy, haphazard farmer who never bothered to make more than a bare living from his small, rundown homestead. He was harmless enough, but he was not a man to be fussy about his personal appearance and cleanliness. He was inclined to talk a lot about nothing. He was known to be slipshod and lazy, and he had trouble finding odd jobs to do in town when his neglected crops didn't pay him enough to keep him clothed and fed.

Because of this, nobody in Dodge ever had much to do with Caleb Weems, except perhaps to nod to him disinterestedly, or perhaps to snicker and make some joke about him, as he rode down Front Street on his barrel-ribbed, bandy-legged old burro.

But it wasn't like that today. Today Caleb Weems was enjoying his hour of glory. For a little while he was the biggest, most sought-after man in Dodge City. It was a new, exciting experience for him and he loved it. He did everything possible to hold his place in the limelight.

Standing next to Caleb Weems for the past hour or so was Mike Galloway. Galloway, who had never been known to do more than sneer at Weems before, now acted as though the old man was his bosom friend. He slapped Weems on the back and prodded him again and again into retelling the details of his story.

The operator of the local land office, Mark Beaumont, a fat, prosperous-looking man in a store-bought coat, clean white shirt, and ribbon tie, upon hearing Weems's story for the first time, said boomingly, "It's a dratted rotten shame, I say, poor old Uncle Jeff dying like that! What kind of a man could do that? I'd like to know." Beaumont pounded the bar for emphasis. "Murder a fine, upstanding citizen like Foster, in cold blood!"

"A man like Jan Gant, that's what kind," Mike Galloway said, wiping his moist mouth with the back of a big, hairy hand. He scowled at the faces of the other men crowded around. "A man who was a hot-tempered killer before he went away from Dodge, who shot one man down in cold blood, even back then. Who spent time in prison learning how to be still more vicious and mean!"

Several of the men in the crowd nodded knowingly. There were murmurs of assent. Then Galloway went on, his closely set, evil-looking eyes too bright and glittery, "It's partly Marshal Dillon's fault that something like this happened. He had warning. I told him that it would. I told him just last night that he ought to run Gant clear out of this part of the country *before* something like this happened."

"You did, Mike?" someone said.

"Sure I did. I was on to Gant as soon as I saw him back

here in town. Any other man who'd disgraced his friends and family wouldn't have had the nerve to come back here—a jailbird who'd been let off too easily for killing a man. He'd have gone somewhere else to start over. But not Jan Gant, mind you! Oh, no. I knew he hadn't come back for any good reason. Why, he probably had this whole thing planned, and that was the *only* reason he came back!"

Seeing that he had a firm hold on his audience, Galloway went on, "But does Marshal Dillon pay any attention to me? Not him. He's too blasted chummy with Gant, if you ask me! So what does he do—and him the local peace officer, mind you!—he personally escorts this killer, this jailbird, Gant, when he rides out to his place. That's the kind of law officer Matt Dillon is, gentlemen!"

Bert Satterfield, a slim middle-aged man who owned the Dodge City Dry Goods Emporium, spoke up, then. His intelligent, gentle-looking eyes steadily on Galloway's, he said softly, "Hold on a moment there, Mike. Matt Dillon might have had good reason to ride out with Gant to his place. He probably wanted to have a long talk with Gant and make sure he wouldn't try to cause any trouble. It would be part of Matt's duty to do something like that."

"Ho-ho!" Galloway roared. "Listen to that, will you,

gentlemen? Good old Matt doin' his duty, eh? Coddlin' a killer and a jailbird!" His coarse laughter cut off suddenly and, his face now ugly with anger at being challenged, he leaned toward Satterfield.

"Well, all I got to say to you, Mr. Storekeeper, is that Dillon sure didn't do much of a job of talkin' Gant out of makin' any trouble. How much more trouble than robbin' and murderin' a poor, harmless, old homesteader can a man make? Eh?"

The crowd murmured in angry agreement again, until Satterfield spoke up, his voice calm and strong, "You're jumping the gun, I'm afraid, Mr. Galloway. We still don't know for sure that Jan Gant did this thing. He hasn't been tried and convicted yet, you know. We haven't any right to prejudge him like this."

"What?" Galloway shouted, raising his fist threateningly. "Gant ran away, didn't he? Ain't that a sign he's guilty? And didn't his own kid break away from Doc Adams and run to join his old man? Didn't he? Ask Caleb Weems there!"

Weems puffed himself up, thrusting his thumbs under dirty, worn galluses, and nodded his head wisely. "That's right, boys," he said. "I saw it with my own two eyes.

Heard him with my own two ears yell back to Doc that he was goin' to run away with his pa!"

"And who else could have done it, Satterfield?" Galloway demanded, thumping his forefinger into the smaller man's chest. "Who lives right there handy, less'n half a mile from Foster—Heaven rest his soul. Who'd Foster let in to visit him late at night—a stranger? And ain't it a mighty long coincidence that this should happen the first night Jan Gant is home from prison?"

"That's all circumstantial evidence only, Galloway," Satterfield persisted.

Some of the older men in the crowd, the obviously more solid citizens, nodded thoughtfully at that. Especially when Satterfield continued, "And you're forgetting all about that hardcase stranger came to town yesterday, Mike. The one you said was called Huggins. Why couldn't he have been the killer? Actually, it could be almost anybody. A lot of people in this town knew Jeff Foster kept a small fortune hidden somewhere out at his place. Plenty of men in this town who wouldn't draw the line at murder for several thousand dollars. In my opinion I think we ought to wait and hear what Gant has to say for himself, what his story is, when Dillon brings him in. Maybe he can clear himself."

"Huh!" Galloway snorted. "You're talkin' like a fool, Satterfield! Sure, maybe this Huggins did have something to do with it. He sure looked to me like a gent who could be capable of killin' his own brother for a few dollars. But if he did, you can bet your boots Jan Gant was in on it with him. Didn't Huggins tell me he'd been Gant's cell mate in the territorial prison and that he'd stopped off in Dodge just to see him? They could have even planned this thing together, when they were in prison!"

The angry mumbling of agreement that greeted that statement prevented Bert Satterfield's answer from being heard. Then Mike Galloway quieted the crowd down by waving his arms and shouting, "Listen a moment! Listen to me, men!"

When the group had quieted, he went on, "I, for one, am fixin' right now to go up and wait in front of the jail-house for the Marshal's return. If he brings Gant in alive, I'm goin' to let that killer know what this town thinks of a man who'd commit a cowardly crime like that against a friend and neighbor who'd helped his wife and boy run their spread while he was in jail. Are any of you with me?"

There were wild hurrahs and whoops of agreement.

Galloway started to push through the mob toward the

door, saying, "We'd better not lose any more time in gettin' up there, then. If Dillon gets back with his prisoner before we get there, he'll lock him up all nice and comfy in a cell and feed him a lot of good meals at the town's expense and we won't even have a chance to let the murderin' weasel know what we think of him! Let's go, men!"

As the crowd pushed and milled about Galloway, following him out, Bert Satterfield and several other business men stepped aside and went over and sat down at a table.

Satterfield shook his head worriedly. "Gentlemen," he said, "I don't much care for the way that Galloway is talking. He's just about got Gant tried and convicted with that gang of town loafers. They could cause real trouble."

"What kind of trouble, Bert?"

"Well, I hate to say it, gentlemen, but I've seen lynch mobs formed by a bunch not even as riled up as that crowd. Not right away, perhaps, but as time goes on and they get to thinking more and more about what a good, kind, grand old man Uncle Jeff Foster was, and how he helped out the Gant woman and her son while Jan was in prison. Especially if Mike Galloway insists on proddin' them that way."

"Oh, you worry too much, Bert," one of the others said.

"Matt Dillon won't let them hang any prisoner of his without a fair trial."

"You ever see a lynch mob in action, Henry?"

The other man shook his head.

"Pretty hard for one man—even a man like Matt Dillon, who has the help of a couple of deputies—to handle an angry mob all fired up to hang somebody. I tell you, if any of us can do anything to stop such a thing, we'd better do it. Keep our heads and try to talk others in town into doing the same. If a lynch mob does form, they'll go crazy as a herd of locoed buffalo. They'll likely wreck the town. And a lynching is always bad for a town. Dodge will have a hard time living it down."

"Well," drawled another man, "mebbe Dillon won't even catch up with Gant. And that'll be the end of it."

Satterfield shook his head knowingly. "Matt Dillon will bring him back. He's never gone out after a man yet, that he failed. . . ."

About fifteen minutes later Marshal Dillon, Chester, Jan Gant, and Tommy rode down the north end of Front Street. As they moved along, dust-covered and weary from the long ride, their horses lathered, Matt Dillon noticed that

in front of every shop, as word of their arrival spread along
the street, men and women gathered, to stare with a cold,
horrified curiosity at Jan Gant. All eyes were on him.

"Sure looks like the news has spread, Mr. Dillon," Chester whispered.

"Yeah. And by the looks on their faces, most of these
folks aren't going to take too smartly to the possibility of
Gant being innocent."

"They sure aren't," Chester answered.

As if in confirmation, one of a group of slovenly looking
men standing in front of a cheap restaurant shook his fist
as they rode past and shouted, "See to it the dirty killer gets
what's coming to him, Marshal!"

At that, Jan Gant turned and looked back, started to
rein in. His face was bleak and flushed with anger. Swiftly
Marshal Dillon rode up beside him and caught his arm.
"Don't pay any attention, Jan," he said. "Just ride on. Keep
your eyes straight ahead and don't even look at them."

"But, Marshal, they've got no right to say things like
that, in front of Tommy, especially. I'm not a killer and I—"

"Hold it, Jan," Dillon cut in. "Do as I say. Trying to
fight back isn't going to change the way they feel. They'll
change their tune fast enough when we get the real killer.

Insults can't really hurt you."

"The Marshal's right," Tommy said, then. "Remember you told me that you'd learned to control your temper?"

"All right, Tommy—Marshal," Gant said. "Let's ride on."

"Before we do," Dillon said, "maybe it would be better if Tommy slid off from behind you, Gant, and rode the rest of the way on Chester's horse."

"It's all right, Marshal," Tommy said quickly. "I'm not ashamed to ride with Pa. I'm stickin' right with him."

"That's brave of you, Tommy, but that isn't why I want you to get down from there and ride with Chester. The way the people here in town seem to be riled up, no telling what might happen. Some loco fool, trying to be important, might decide to chunk a rock at your pa or something. No sense in giving them a bigger target or taking a chance on your getting hurt."

"I hadn't thought about that, Marshal," Jan Gant said. "And see there, down by the jailhouse! Looks like quite a crowd has formed a reception committee for us. Just in case there is bad trouble, Tommy, do as the Marshal says."

Obediently, Tommy slid from the horse and went over to Chester, who helped him fork up behind him.

They rode on. As they neared the front of the jailhouse, they saw a crowd of fifteen or twenty rough-looking men, standing close together in the middle of the street, blocking their approach.

Dillon said, "Chester, from here on, do exactly as I tell you and the instant I tell you. Understand? I think I can handle this bunch without any real trouble breaking out, but it's liable to be touch and go. If I tell you to halt, Chester, halt, pronto. If I say, ride, keep going, no matter who might be in the way."

"Yes, sir," Chester said, his Adam's apple moving nervously. His eyes grew very large. "You mean even if I have to ride somebody down, Mr. Dillon?"

"I don't think they'll let you do that. But they may try to bluff us unless we show them we won't be bluffed. . . . Chester, you ride up in front of Gant. I'll ride behind him."

To Gant, Dillon said, "I'll see that nobody touches you, Jan. But please do as I say. If you don't do exactly as I say, violence may flare up and Tommy could get hurt bad, as well as other people. So if you think anything of him, do exactly as I tell you. You hear?"

His voice so deep and low it could scarcely be heard, Jan Gant said, "All right, Marshal. Anything to keep Tommy safe. What do you want me to do?"

"Keep your gaze over the heads of the crowd. Don't look at their faces. And no matter what they do or say, don't you make a move. Just sit that horse and be quiet. No matter what they say to you—or to Tommy. Is that clear?"

Jan Gant nodded. He hunched his big shoulders, and his huge hands gripped the reins so tightly that his knuckles showed whitely through the skin.

"All right," Dillon said. "Let's go."

The undertone of talk among the crowd in the street began to swell as the four of them rode closer. Now Marshal Dillon saw Mike Galloway in the front of the crowd, angrily talking to men on either side of him, gesturing wildly with his thick arms.

"I would have bet it was Galloway," Dillon said. Then he shouted, "Galloway, are you the leader of this bunch?"

The crowd went suddenly silent. Grinning, folding his arms across his chest, Galloway answered, "Nobody's the leader, Marshal. We just happen to be a group of good citizens of Dodge, all of the same mind—the same opinion."

"I just want to make sure you understand, Galloway," Dillon told him, "if there's any trouble, I'm going to hold you personally responsible."

"Trouble, Marshal? Now, we ain't fixin' to make any trouble for you. We've just been waitin' here to pay our respects to your killer-jailbird friend, Jan Gant. It was good of you to bring him back. I'm surprised you didn't make sure he got clean away."

The crowd was right in front of them, then. Marshal Dillon looked carefully at their faces, noting who was there. He was happy to see that most of them were town loafers, riff-raff from the other side of the Deadline, the kind that usually could be found around a loud-talking bully like Galloway.

"You men get out of my way," Dillon told them. "You're blocking the street. I've got a prisoner to take in and I aim to do it."

"Oh?" Galloway sneered. "You mean you're lockin' Gant up, Marshal? We kind of thought you might be fixin' to put him up at the Dodge House—in the Royal Suite, maybe."

There was a roar of rude laughter from the other men. Galloway looked around him proudly. He and the rest of the men still stood their ground although Chester, white-faced now, leading the group on horseback, was almost on top of the crowd.

Suddenly Dillon called, "Hold it, Chester. Halt!"

Chester reined in so suddenly that Gant's horse, right behind him, had to veer.

Marshal Dillon said, "All right, Galloway, we don't want any trouble with you or your bunch. Speak your piece quickly, then get out of our way."

"Why, sure, Marshal." A sly look slid across Galloway's beefy face. He wet his lips nervously and glanced quickly at Dillon's right hand, resting close to the butt of his forty-four.

"But don't you get any idea of drawin' that gun on us, Marshal," Galloway went on. "I'm sure these gents with me wouldn't cater none to that. They might decide to kill you *and* that thievin', murderin' coyote you're protectin' so cozy. Y'hear, Marshal?"

"If you or this mob starts trouble with me, you'll take the consequences," Dillon told him. "Now, get out of the way. This is the last time I'll tell you. If you don't move, we'll ride over you."

"I don't reckon you'd really do that, Marshal," Galloway said. Then he pointed at Jan Gant. "Look at him, men, look at the jailbird-killer sittin' up there—high 'n' mighty, ain't he? Won't even look at us. Like maybe he thinks he's too good for us, him bein' such a bold, bad outlaw who kills harmless ol' men!"

With that, Mike Galloway, his face red with rage and blue veins standing at his temples, moved closer to Jan Gant. The others jostled each other nervously, following him.

"What's the matter, Gant?" Galloway demanded. "I thought you was supposed to be such a hardcase. Even gave me a bad time once in a fight. Of course, you fought dirty as a sidewinder to do it. But how come you sit there, now, so biggety and take insults? Huh, Gant, you old-man-killer?"

Suddenly Tommy Gant cried, "You stop talkin' like that to my pa, Mr. Galloway! You stop it! He isn't a killer and Marshal Dillon's goin' to prove it!"

Galloway laughed. He pointed at Tommy. "You hear that, gents? You hear the jailbird's kid stickin' up for him after he killed the nice old feller who took care of the boy all the time his old man was in prison? Maybe it's like they say, eh? Like father, like son. Mebbe he'll grow up to be a sneakin' neighbor-killer just like his pa, huh?"

Tears of rage stung Tommy's eyes, almost blinding him. He started to shout something back but then Chester said sharply, "Tommy, you hush, you hear?" And Chester reached around and slapped him smartly on the thigh.

Marshal Dillon looked at Jan Gant's white, rigid face and the cords standing out with strain, at his neck. He knew Gant couldn't take much more of this abuse. Dillon said, "All right, Galloway, you and your friends have had your say, now get out of the way! Start moving, Chester. If they keep blocking the way, there's nothing you can do but ride 'em down. We've warned them enough."

Chester urged his mount forward slowly. Galloway and the others, still grinning and leering, stood their ground for a moment, but then as Chester's horse kept moving forward, at the last possible moment they broke up and made an open path for the riders to move through.

7   *Showdown at the Long Branch*

After they had hitched their horses outside the jailhouse, Marshal Dillon opened the door, led the others inside, and locked it again. Chester grinned at him admiringly.

"Jumpin' catfish, Mr. Dillon, you sure did have that crowd sized up right. When the time came, they just backed out of the way like a speckled pup who's just been nicked on the nose by a tough ol' tomcat."

"You sure did, Marshal," Tommy said, looking a little sheepish. "But I'm sorry I didn't obey orders and spoke out of turn."

Dillon smiled at him warmly. "That's all right, Tommy. I'm surprised you did as well as you did under the circumstances. And I'm right proud of the way your pa held a checkrein on himself. Don't know whether I could have done the same if things like that were bein' said about me."

"I almost busted loose a couple of times, Marshal," Gant admitted. "But I'm glad now that I didn't. That's what they were waitin' for, I suspect. That would have given them all an excuse to jump me, yank me off that horse."

"Well, we won the first round anyhow," Dillon said.

Chester frowned. "The first round?"

"Could be that bunch is just gettin' warmed up, Chester. Especially if they can get a lot of other folks in town feelin' the same way they do. I expect we'll be hearing more from them."

Just then there was a knock on the door. Dillon stepped toward it, said, "Who's there?"

"Me—Doc Adams. Who in tarnation you think it is? Open up and let me in."

"Sure thing, Doc." Dillon unlocked the door and Doc Adams came bustling in, yanking off his hat and throwing it onto a table. He pushed his hand through his rumpled gray hair, looking around at Jan and Tommy Gant. He said hello to them both and then turned to Dillon.

"That bunch of hoodlums out there give you any trouble, Matt?"

"Some."

"What are they up to? With that Mike Galloway frontin'

'em, can't be anything good."

"Just wanted to do a little pickin' at Jan Gant, Doc."

Doc Adams looked at Jan and Tommy Gant for a moment, as he fidgeted uncomfortably and tugged with his thumb and forefinger at the loose, whiskered skin at his throat.

"Soon as I heard you were back, I rushed right down, Matt," he said, then. "Got something you ought to know." He jerked his head meaningly at the Gants. "Sort of private-like."

"All right." Dillon moved to the far side of the room, and when Doc joined him, he said in a low voice, "What's on your mind, Doc?"

"Plenty," Adams said. "And all bad. But first, tell me what the situation is with him." He nodded his head. "Your prisoner there."

As briefly as possible, Dillon explained everything, telling of his theory about the man called Huggins. When he had finished, Doc Adams nodded sagely. Then he coughed apologetically behind his hand and his tired but wise-looking eyes held Dillon's searchingly.

"I sure hope it turns out that way, Matt. After you left this morning and while I was riding back to town, I kept thinking about it. I wondered how a man like Gant could do something like that. I kept telling myself that he couldn't, hadn't. Yet there was strong evidence. . . ."

Doc Adams broke off for a moment and then said, "This business about it being Huggins, and Gant clear out of it, Matt? Is that the heart or the head talkin'?"

Dillon snorted and looked away briefly. "Doc, you know I don't have a heart. After all my years as a peace officer in a town like Dodge, how could I?"

"Dodge isn't so bad," Doc snapped. "And you don't fool me any, Matt Dillon. Underneath that great, hulkin', beefy, tough hide of yours, you're probably the biggest softy in town. I swear I don't know sometimes how you even make a success of this law-enforcin' business."

From the other side of the room, Chester called, "Hey, what are you two whisperin' about like a couple of gossipy old ladies?"

"Mind your business, young feller," Doc told him tartly.

Chester tipped his hat back on his head and snickered. "Well, listen to old Doc, will you? Grouchy as a cat with new kittens just because nobody was thoughtful enough to break a leg or run a nail through their foot or somethin', within the last twenty-four hours."

Doc scowled ferociously at Chester and said hotly, "Some day somebody'll run a nail through that foolish tongue of yours, Chester, to stop it from flappin' all the time. Why don't you just go and weigh down your mind with some of those mail-order pamphlets for kids that you prize so highly, and let Matt and me finish talkin'?"

"That's an idea, Chester," Dillon said. "Why don't you let Tommy take a look at those books? He'll probably get a kick out of them."

"Sure thing, Mr. Dillon." Chester went to the desk and started hunting for the pamphlets.

His voice lowered once again, Doc Adams said, "Matt, what I came to tell you is that Mrs. Gant is here in town. She's back."

"What?" Dillon gasped.

Doc put his finger to his lips. "Keep your voice down. It may be best for Gant not to know this. The boy, either."

"But, how'd she—"

"Well, there's a stage stop in the town near where Mrs. Gant's been convalescing, resting while her health improves. Last night some idiot from town here, don't know offhand who it was, took the stage up there on business. And the husband of Mrs. Hopkins—the woman takin' care of Mrs.

Gant—works in the stage station. He heard the man from town here talking about Jan Gant being home and then went home and told Mrs. Hopkins. Mrs. Gant overheard this. She couldn't wait, then, to get home. She insisted on leaving early this morning, before dawn. Mrs. Hopkins, who rode in with her, told me she insisted that Mrs. Gant wait until I gave the word it was all right for her to travel. But Mrs. Gant couldn't wait. She had to come."

"I see," Dillon said. He stroked his chin thoughtfully, looking across the room at Jan Gant. "What happened when she got here? Did the traveling bother her?"

"Some, Matt. But I reckon the idea of seein' her husband again, having him home with her once more, was the best medicine she could have had. She was pale and peaked lookin', mind you, but not as much as I would have expected after that trip."

"You told her—about Uncle Jeff Foster, Doc?"

Doc Adams cracked his knuckles angrily. Looking down at them, he muttered, "What else could I do, Matt? Naturally I tried to break it to her as gentle as I could." He looked up at Dillon, then, his old eyes pleading for understanding. "I had no choice, Matt. The news was already all over town. She would have heard it in some worse fashion, soon enough. And how could I stop her from goin' on out home and wantin' to see Uncle Jeff when she got there? I just had no choice, by thunder! You know that, Matt!"

"I can see where you wouldn't have. How'd she take it, Doc? Real bad?"

"Couldn't have been any worse. Now, if everything had been all right when she got here, Matt, that trip probably wouldn't have taken any toll of her. But on top of that strain, the shock of this news was too much. You know how much she thought of old Uncle Jeff after all he's done for her and the boy. Well, with it bein' him, and her husband suspected—it was too much for the poor woman. She went into a state of shock and then had a bad relapse."

"Where is she now?"

"Nearest place I figured she'd be comfortable, Matt. I took her to Mrs. Biddy McCue's boardinghouse—you know, the place Chester's livin' right now. Her rooms are big and airy and her food's good. Mrs. Hopkins couldn't stay on with her, but Mrs. Biddy's a smart hand with a sick person."

Dillon looked toward the Gants. "You think he ought to know, Doc?"

"I didn't think so, when I first came in. Now I've changed my mind. It'll do her good to have the boy with her, so I guess we'll have to tell them."

"She will get well again, won't she, Doc?"

Adams looked away. He tugged at his mustache. "That depends. Having something like she's got on her mind right now isn't helping any."

"Would it help if her husband is cleared of all suspicion?"

"Of course it would, if that happens soon enough, Matt. By the same token, if it turns out the other way and you're all wrong about Gant, I wouldn't be responsible for whatever might happen to her."

Marshal Dillon sucked in a deep breath. "All right, Doc. Let's get Jan over here and tell him first. Then he can break the news to the boy, maybe tell him what to say to his mother."

"Now you're thinkin' for a change, Matt," Doc said. "It's a wonder you didn't elect me for the unpleasant job of telling the boy."

As they called Jan Gant over to them, Dillon saw that Tommy was holding Chester's mail-order pamphlets in his hand, while he and Chester looked at some of the Wanted dodgers on the wall of the office.

Later, after Doc Adams had taken Tommy Gant to be with his mother, Dillon locked Jan Gant into a cell and the big man sprawled on the bunk and almost instantly fell into the deep sleep of exhaustion.

Dillon wrote his report on what had happened at the Foster place, as best he knew it, then got up from his desk and picked up his hat.

"Chester, I've got some business to tend to outside. Don't leave here under any circumstances, until I get back. I don't think that Galloway bunch will try to break in here, but we can't take any chances. Even though I'll be keeping their ringleader busy for a while."

Chester, who had been sitting on a chair tilted back against the wall and had been dozing lightly, rubbed his eyes.

"You goin' to talk to Mike, Mr. Dillon? What about?"

"Not much point in telling you until I get back, Chester. I just got a wild idea. There might not be anything to it."

"You be gone very long?"

"Why?"

"Well, nothin', Mr. Dillon, only it's past noon already and . . . ." Chester let the words trail off and put a hand over his stomach.

Dillon grinned. "You won't die of starvation before I get back. I'll bring you some chow. . . . So long, Chester. Try to stay awake."

"Oh, you know I will, Mr. Dillon."

At the door, Dillon glanced around and grinned. Chester's eyes were already heavy-lidded again.

Marshal Dillon walked down the street to the Long Branch. He went inside and glanced at the crowd. It included nearly all the men who had been with Galloway earlier, and a lot of others, three deep at the bar. They were making a good deal of noise, but it was not the sound of men enjoying themselves in harmlessly letting off steam. There was a sinister undertone to the voices.

Kitty, the woman who owned the Long Branch, came over to Dillon. Her pretty eyes held sympathy and understanding as she said, "Hello, Matt. Sorry to hear about the trouble you're caught up in. I hated hearing about Uncle Jeff Foster, of course. I liked him. Everybody did. You couldn't help it."

"I know, Kitty," Dillon answered. "That's the trouble."

"I know, too, how something like this upsets you, Matt, until you get the man who did it. Is Gant the one, the way everybody's saying?"

"I don't know for sure, Kitty. I think not. Maybe I'm just *hoping* not, on account of his missus and their boy. There is a good bit of circumstantial evidence against Gant, of course."

"Is that all?" Kitty looked surprised. She pushed a loose strand of curly hair up into place. "The way that bunch at the bar's been talkin', I figured you probably even had witnesses that saw Gant do it. That Galloway bunch has Gant practically hanged for the deed already."

"That's what Galloway would like to see happen, all right," Dillon answered. "And that's what I want to talk to him about. If you'll excuse me, Kitty. . . ."

As Dillon walked toward the bar, somebody saw him approaching Galloway and the loud talking quickly died out. A lot of the men looked coldly at Dillon. Mike Galloway swung around and hooked his elbows over the bar.

"Well, Marshal," Galloway began in the kind of soft, respectful voice that didn't belong with the sneer around his mouth, "how soon we goin' to have the trial? Some of these gents are mighty impatient to see Jan Gant swing for what he did, Marshal."

"I guess you could be one of those, Galloway, eh?"

"Why, sure, I like to see justice done, Marshal. Every

law-abidin' citizen does. Especially when a nice, harmless old man like Uncle Jeff was the victim of the killer."

"I see." Dillon hooked his thumbs into his gun belt. "But you wouldn't have any special interest in having Gant convicted and hung fast, would you, Galloway?"

The other man looked puzzled for a moment. "I might. I can't help I don't love the man like you do, Marshal."

Dillon held tight to his temper. After a moment he said, "Yesterday, Galloway, you were plenty scared about Gant being back in town. I don't think I've ever seen a man quite so scared. You don't deny that, do you, that you were frightened out of your hide about Gant being back?"

Red flushed up from Galloway's neckerchief, spread over his face. For a moment his close-set eyes looked sick with shame, but then he blurted, "Sure, I was scared. Of bein' back-shot by a revenge-hungry jailbird. I knew Jan Gant wouldn't think twice about doin' that, first chance he got. Naturally I was anxious for you to run him out of these parts so I wouldn't have to go around all the time never knowin' when a piece of lead was going to slap me between the shoulders."

"You really believed Gant would do that, didn't you, Galloway?"

"I *knew* he would, Marshal. I didn't just believe it."

"Uh-huh. I've been thinking, Galloway, that a man that scared might go to any lengths to remove that fear. He might do anything, just so he could feel safe again. A fear like that is a terrible thing, Galloway. It can make a man pretty desperate."

Galloway frowned. His thick fingers moved nervously against his thighs. "I don't think I get your point, Marshal. What are you gettin' at?"

"You did a lot of talking yesterday and last night, to me—probably to some others, too—about how Gant was going to kill Uncle Jeff Foster. You really drummed that home every chance you got."

"Why, sure!" Galloway looked surprised. "I couldn't have been any more right, could I?"

Dillon ignored that. "The only thing is, it's kind of a giant-sized coincidence that last night Uncle Jeff just happened to be killed. It would almost look as though you knew it was going to happen, Galloway. Now, how could you be so sure of something like that?"

"Same way I was sure Gant'd kill me if he got the chance. Didn't he swear at his trial he'd kill Uncle Jeff? So naturally I—"

"Let me finish, Galloway," Dillon interrupted. "Suppose a man, so deathly afraid of Jan Gant being back, thought up a clever way to get rid of Gant, make sure he'd never have to worry about him again."

"What are you talkin' about, Marshal?" Galloway's eyes began to narrow.

"Suppose this idea of his looked even better when an ex-convict friend of Gant's showed up in town."

"What idea, Marshal?"

"That if this man should go out to Uncle Jeff Foster's during the night and rob and kill Uncle Jeff and then make it look as though Jan Gant did it, there'd be a fine chance that Gant would get the blame for it. That would work fine for this man, two ways. He'd get rid of Gant, a man he'd always hated—and he'd have a small fortune, stolen from Uncle Jeff. A man might think of something like that, mightn't he, Galloway?"

Galloway's fists balled tightly at his sides. He leaned away from the bar, conscious of the sudden silence in the place, the eyes of all the other men on him.

"What man, Marshal? Who are you sayin' did something like that?"

"I didn't say someone did it—I said it could be done."

A slow, smug smile slipped across Galloway's face. "That's better, Marshal. I knew you wouldn't be one to make false accusations like that." He looked around at some of the others and winked. "Besides, Marshal, that idea of yours has a lot of holes in it. What about that tobacco pouch of Gant's found near Uncle Jeff's corpse?"

"This man I was talking about," Dillon answered, "could have seen Vince Huggins with that pouch, seen Gant's initials, and bought the pouch from Huggins, figuring to leave it at the scene of the crime to point to Gant."

"Huh?" Galloway looked puzzled. "What would Huggins be doing with Gant's tobacco pouch?"

"Gant left it behind in his cell and Huggins picked it up."

"Ooooooooooh!" Galloway pretended to be greatly impressed. "So Gant says! So he's tryin' to use an unlikely story like that to pin the whole thing on his pardner, Huggins, is he? Well, that's not very surprisin', Marshal."

"That point can be proved easily enough, when I get in touch with the prison. They'll have a record of the belongings each man took with him when he checked out."

Galloway shrugged and started to turn back to the bar. "Marshal," he said, "I'm gettin' a little tired of all this crazy talk about mysterious people tryin' to frame Gant for the killin'. Everybody in town—except maybe you, Marshal—knows Jan Gant did it. Why don't you go tell your fairy tales to Chester, Marshal? I'm sure he'd appreciate them."

Someone guffawed loudly.

Marshal Dillon reached out and took hold of Galloway's shoulder and spun him roughly around. Galloway's mouth tightened into a thin, ugly seam. "Marshal, you've got no right to manhandle me. Keep your hands off of me."

In a too-soft voice, speaking through clenched teeth, Dillon said, "Galloway, you have the good manners to face me when I'm speaking to you—and answer my questions. You understand that? Don't give me a good excuse to lose my temper with you, Galloway. I'd like nothing better. You've always been a troublemaker in this town."

"I'll answer any sensible questions, Marshal. Just don't put hands on me. You've got no right."

"All right then, Galloway, answer this question. Can you prove where you were all last night?"

"Maybe I can. But why should I? Are you accusing me of something? I don't have to put up with that."

"I'm saying that it wouldn't bother a man like you, Galloway, to kill somebody and make it look like another

man was guilty, just to get revenge on that other man. Especially if there was a lot of money in it for you. . . . Now you tell me where you were all last night, Galloway, and then go with me while I search your room."

"Search my— What for?"

"For the biggest part of Uncle Jeff's stolen savings, the part that still hasn't been found."

"So you *are* accusing me!" Galloway blurted, his face now purple with temper. "Why, you—"

With one hand he pushed himself away from the bar, toward Dillon. With the other, he swung with all his power at Dillon's chin.

The blow never landed. Dillon tipped his head to one side, and at the same time took a half step backward. The punch went harmlessly across his shoulder. Before Galloway could recover his balance, Dillon, with an easy grace that looked almost effortless, swung a short hooking blow to the pit of Galloway's stomach.

Galloway slid down the bar to the floor, holding his stomach, gasping for breath. Dillon stood looking down at him, rubbing the knuckles of his right hand. A moment later, Galloway recovered his breath and got back on his feet. There was no more fight in him, though. He just stood there, staring sullenly at Dillon.

Pain was flashing all through Dillon's right hand, almost numbing it. He wondered, momentarily, how he could have hurt his fist so badly, hitting such a soft part of Galloway's body. He thought that he must have hit the man's belt buckle by mistake. Then he saw that Galloway wasn't wearing a belt; he was using galluses to hold up his trousers.

The pain in his hand began to ease then, and Dillon forgot about it as Galloway said grudgingly, "Sorry, Marshal. I shouldn't have swung at you like that. But you got me pretty upset, accusin' me of—listen, Marshal, I've got nothing to hide. You're on the wrong trail. I can prove where I was every minute of last night. And if you want to, you can come search my room. Only bring another man along as a witness, so you can't plant anything there."

Dillon looked searchingly at Galloway and saw that the man wasn't bluffing. The Marshal began to feel a little foolish.

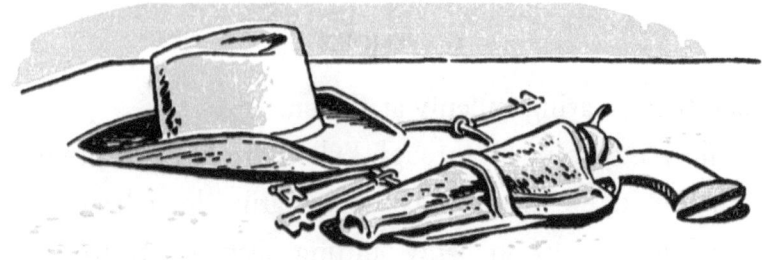

8   A New Suspect

It was nearly two o'clock in the afternoon when Marshal Dillon got back to the jailhouse. He remembered to stop by the O. K. Cafe and have a couple of lunches put up for himself and Chester. With his mind busy on other things, he forgot about bringing a meal for their prisoner. It didn't make any difference. Jan Gant was still sleeping.

Watching Chester eat, Dillon grinned and said, "Chester, you always eat as though it's going to be your last meal on earth and it's been a long time since the one before."

Chester paused with a forkful of food halfway to his mouth. "Well, it has been a long time, Mr. Dillon. I haven't had a bite since about five o'clock this morning."

"Don't tell me that. You always eat that way, Chester. I've watched you before."

Chester swallowed another mouthful of food. "Well, I

suppose it isn't very polite, Mr. Dillon, but leastways folks always know I enjoy my food."

"Sometimes I wonder, the way you gulp it. It isn't just the politeness, Chester, but it's a wonder you don't get a stomach-ache, swallowing it down practically whole that way. Don't you know that's not good for you?"

"I know it," Chester admitted, eating just as fast as before. "I guess I'm just a growing boy, eh, Mr. Dillon?"

The Marshal laughed. After a moment Chester said, "Where'd you go before and what was the idea you were workin' on?"

"It blew up in my face, Chester. I suppose that's what I get for letting my personal dislike of a man make me suspicious of him. It wasn't very professional of me."

Then Dillon told Chester how he had begun to suspect Galloway, for being so positive beforehand that Uncle Jeff Foster would be killed, and then, today, because of the way he had tried to incite the mob against Gant. He related the scene at the Long Branch.

When he told about hitting Galloway, Chester stared at Dillon's hand and said, "Goodness sakes, Mr. Dillon, he sure must've had a hard stomach. Your hand's even swollen a little around the knuckles."

Dillon looked down at it. "I can't figure that out."

Then Chester said, "So Galloway was able to prove where he was all last night, eh? After he left that poker game, late, he went with that weird character they call Jumbo Jones, out to his shack and spent the night there? How come he did that, Mr. Dillon? Why didn't he sleep in his own room in town?"

"He claimed he did it because he was afraid Jan Gant might try to kill him in his sleep, Chester. Whatever reason, that's what he did, all right."

"Jumbo Jones swore to it, huh? He could have been lying, Mr. Dillon. That Jumbo thinks Galloway is so wonderful, he'd do anything for him. Galloway could lie and Jumbo would swear to it. Isn't that so?"

"Yes, ordinarily, Chester. But Jumbo isn't cunning enough to lie well. He's tried it before and I've always been able to tell in a few minutes. I questioned Jumbo upside down and sideways, Chester, and he wasn't lying, I know. He claimed Galloway went home with him and spent the night there. So that's it."

"How about searching Galloway's room?"

"I didn't bother, Chester. I was going to, but Galloway was too willing. He wasn't bluffing, either. He was almost anxious for me to do it, so he could have a big laugh on me, I guess. I know I wouldn't have found anything there."

"Then that about eliminates Galloway as a possible suspect, doesn't it, Mr. Dillon?"

"I'm afraid so, Chester."

"That's a shame. You know, I never have liked that man, Mr. Dillon."

"I know, Chester. It's a hard thing to do."

"What is?"

"Like a man of Galloway's cut. . . ." Dillon finished his lunch and got up. "Well, there isn't much of the afternoon left, Chester. I've got a lot to do."

"Where you goin', Mr. Dillon?"

"I thought I'd ride out to the river bottom section and snoop around a little at some of the other homesteads. Ask a few questions, maybe. You know, we still can't rule out the possibility that we've gotten off on the wrong track altogether. Almost everybody in that area knew about Uncle Jeff's money being hidden around his house. Somebody out there may have had a yen to get hold of that money for some time and, when Jan Gant came back, figured it was a good time to strike and pin the blame on an ex-convict."

"What about that tobacco pouch, Mr. Dillon? That sort of narrows it down to either Gant or—if he was telling the truth about it—Huggins. Doesn't it?"

"I've been thinking about that. Not necessarily, Chester. Huggins, if he did have that pouch, could have dropped it somewhere, lost it, one way or another."

"I hadn't thought about that."

"Well, hold things down tight, Chester. If Gant's hungry when he wakes, slip out and get him some grub. But make sure you lock the door, when you do."

"I'll take care of everything, Mr. Dillon."

"I'll try to be back by sundown, Chester."

Out on the street, Marshal Dillon became aware that not much work was getting done in Dodge this day. Business men and their customers were gathered outside most of the stores in little groups. Everybody stared curiously at Dillon as he rode by. Most of them only nodded in stiff recognition of his greeting. It looked as though perhaps Galloway's talk, about Dillon protecting Gant too much, was beginning to have some effect.

Then, instead of passing the Long Branch, where one of Galloway's bunch would probably see him, Dillon cut down a side street and left town by a different route. He didn't like the idea of that bunch knowing he was out of town.

Out near the river bottom country, Marshal Dillon made his first stop at the homestead of a family named Nichols. Their place was in back of Uncle Jeff Foster's. It was a small spread that had obviously been worked hard but hadn't produced very well. The house was nothing more than roughly timbered walls and roof, with sod patches on the roof, built against a sharply cut embankment. The embankment formed the rear wall of the house.

In the unfenced yard, two small girls were playing a hopscotch game and paused in their play only to take a quick look and recognize Dillon, when he rode into the yard. Near the girls a tethered goat eyed the marshal suspiciously as he hitched his horse to the rail.

Dillon stood for a moment and looked at the children. Their dresses were neatly sewn together but obviously made out of flour sacks. Both little girls were pitifully thin. Looking at them and then at the crude house and the poor-looking crops in the fields to the right, Dillon thought that as badly as the Nicholses needed money, it wouldn't be surprising if the father committed some desperate act.

Yet Dillon knew Jacob Nichols never would. He was

too proud a man even to borrow or accept help from anyone. Several people had tried to help the Nicholses from time to time. They had been turned down politely but firmly.

Dillon spoke to the girls. They both turned and flashed him quick smiles. Almost in unison, they said, "Marshal."

At the door of the house, Mrs. Nichols was already standing waiting for Dillon. He took off his hat. Mrs. Nichols was a small, frail-looking woman with enormous dark eyes and prematurely gray hair. She tilted her head forward stiffly and said, "Evenin', Marshal. My mister's not to home, so I can't ask you in. He doesn't like me to have anyone in when he's not here. He's down at the river fishing."

"I'm sorry to trouble you, Mrs. Nichols," Dillon said. "I wanted to talk to you about the tragedy over at Uncle Jeff Foster's place."

Mrs. Nichols bowed her head. "It's too bad," she said softly. "He was a good man, they say. We didn't know him too well. We just aren't over-neighborly people, I reckon, Marshal. What'd you want to talk about?"

"Well, your place is fairly close to his, and I was just wonderin' if you or Mr. Nichols might have heard any riders goin' through this way late last night."

"No, sir. If we did, we wouldn't have studied 'em. We

let other folks be, if they let us be."

"Have you heard anything around this section—I mean, do folks who live around Uncle Jeff have any ideas about who might have done such a thing?"

She shook her head. "Uh-uh, Marshal. We don't do much visitin'—don't have many visitors, neither. Afraid I can't tell you anything, Marshal. Sorry."

The interview was obviously over. Dillon backed away from the door, thanking Mrs. Nichols for her trouble. Riding away from the place, he wondered if he would have the same trouble everywhere. Would all these river bottom people be so closemouthed? He had an idea that even if Mrs. Nichols had known anything, he never would have been able to pry it out of her.

At the next place he stopped, Dillon passed a corral where a boy of about twelve was trying to break a beautiful Indian pony to the saddle. The boy would stay seated for several seconds until the pony sunfished too hard for him, and then he would pitch off into the soft dirt of the corral. Each time it happened, a shriveled-looking little man, hardly taller than the twelve-year-old boy, would laugh until he almost doubled over.

Dillon caught the man's attention between fits of laughter. "Evenin', Mr. Appleyard. Your boy's not going to let that pony outspunk him, is he?"

"No, sirree, Marshal, he ain't about to," the little man said. "Richie's a good, stout lad. Takes after his daddy, of course." Appleyard roared with laughter at the joke on himself.

In the corral, Richie Appleyard picked himself up from the turf once again, shaking his head ruefully. When he looked toward the marshal, Dillon called, "That's goin' to make a fine ridin' pony, Rich, when you finally get him settled down."

"Yes, sir," the boy said, grinning, obviously pleased.

Leaning on the fence, Dillon said, "Mr. Appleyard, what do you know, if anything, about what happened to Uncle Jeff Foster?" He thought he would try the direct approach this time.

Appleyard looked sharply at Dillon for a moment. "Now, what makes you think I might know somethin', Marshal? I don't like to get anybody into trouble. Not even that miserable Nick Root."

Dillon concealed his surprise just in time. It seemed that his direct approach had led Appleyard to assume that the Marshal knew he had some information.

"I need all the help I can get on this one, Mr. Appleyard," Dillon said. "Hopin' something will turn up that'll let me turn loose Jan Gant." Dillon knew that before Gant was sent away he and Appleyard had been friendly.

"Ought to turn him loose right now," Appleyard said decisively. "Know that man didn't do it. Couldn't. No matter how bad it looks. Sure he killed that gunman feller in Dodge, way back. But that's a heap different than killin' a helpless old man who's your good neighbor, then stealin' from him. Man doesn't change, Marshal—been to prison or not. Jan Gant never was the kind of man to be able to do a thing like that. Never will be."

"Trouble is," Dillon said quickly, hoping to catch Appleyard off guard, "that there isn't a bit of evidence that points to anyone else—outside of a stranger to these parts, called Huggins."

"Weren't that Huggins I heard about neither," Appleyard said. He bent and picked up a piece of yard dirt and crumpled it between his fingers. "Least I don't think so. Well, maybe it's sinful to get somebody else into trouble, but I'm goin' to give you some evidence that points to somebody beside Jan Gant, Marshal."

Just then a woman's deeply booming voice called from

the neat, newly painted farmhouse behind them, "Julian? Who's that out there with you?"

Dillon turned and waved to Mrs. Appleyard, standing in the doorway of the house. She was such a big woman that she almost filled the whole doorway. She was at least a head taller than Mr. Appleyard and some eighty or a hundred pounds heavier. When the two came into Dodge together, people who didn't know them immediately felt sorry for Appleyard and assumed that he was henpecked and had few rights of his own with such a big-built woman for a wife. Actually, it was just the opposite.

Appleyard frowned, annoyed. Impatiently he shouted back, "It's only the Marshal and me, havin' a little talk, Ida. Now, you get back there in that house and mind your business, my love!"

"Yes, Julian," his wife's strong, deep voice answered. Instantly she disappeared into the dimness of the house.

"Let a woman get nosy," Appleyard said, "no tellin' how far she'll get to pryin' in a man's business. Ain't that so, Marshal?"

Dillon grinned. "I'm not much of an authority, Mr. Appleyard. Never been married."

"Take my word for it, Marshal. . . . Now what was it

we were talkin' about before my woman interrupted?"

"Nick Root," Dillon said. "You think he knows anything about what happened to Uncle Jeff?"

"I don't know, Marshal. Tell you what I *do* know though and let you draw your own conclusions. You know what a sorry scoundrel that Nick Root is, don't you? I mean him never havin' done a lick of work in his life and livin' down in that fishin' shack on the creek, all by himself except for those two big, vicious dogs of his."

Dillon nodded, wishing Appleyard would get to the point. But he knew better than to try to hurry the man. If he did that and Appleyard became hurt, he might not give out another word of information.

Appleyard shook his head despairingly. "Mean as a snake, too, that Nick Root feller. You heard about him killin' a man with his bare hands, over to Abilene, didn't you?"

"I heard something about it. What's all this got to do with Uncle Jeff?"

"I'm comin' to that, Marshal. Just keep your shirttail in. ... Anyhow, on top of everything, Root's been stealin' from us homesteaders around here for years."

Dillon raised his eyebrows. "Nobody ever reported it."

"No, I don't reckon so, Marshal, but that don't change the fact. He's slick, this Nick Root. Nobody's ever caught him at it. The stealin', I mean. Yet it's been goin' on. And ain't nobody else it could be. He'll take a couple of chickens from this one, some eggs from another. Take some meat from another man's smoke house. Things like that. He's slick enough to realize that if he doesn't take too much at one time from one person, they're less likely to make a fuss about it. One reason, along with the fact nobody's ever caught him red-handed, that he's never been reported.

"But that's only petty thievery, Marshal," Appleyard went on, after pausing to knock some caked mud from between the heel and sole of his boot. "Either last night or early today, though, this Nick Root's stumbled onto something big."

Dillon's interest quickened. "What do you mean?"

"Well, Nick Root's never had more than two pennies to rub together in his whole life. But I had occasion to be in Dodge this mornin' on business—had to go to a little metal-smith shop the other side of the Deadline—and who do you think I spotted comin' out of one of those Texas Street deadfall dives, Marshal, big as life?"

"Nick Root."

"None other. But that ain't all. In his hand, Nick is holding a whole fistful of greenbacks. And he's all dressed up in a brand-new suit too. He was sure raisin' cane on a Christmas tree, too, Marshal, havin' himself a *big* time. . . . But on whose money, Marshal?"

"Uh-huh," Dillon said. "Maybe I'd better go have a talk with Mr. Nick Root."

"You do that, sir. If that ain't Uncle Jeff Foster's money that man's spendin', I'll eat my own hat. Listen, Marshal, I gave him a ride back from town one day—felt sorry even for a no-'count like him, havin' to walk so far in that broiling sun—and when we passed Uncle Jeff's place, he did nothing but talk about all the cash he'd heard Uncle Jeff had hidden around the place and how he could sure use a lot of money like that. I remembered that quite plain this morning, when I saw him and realized he'd obviously come into a lot of money. It all came back to me right clear, Marshal, and I told myself—"

"Much obliged to you," Dillon broke in. "It does sound as though Nick Root might be the one. You did right, telling me about this, Mr. Appleyard."

"Well, I don't know, sir. My woman, she tried to tell me I should mind my own business. But the way I look on it,

Marshal, if Nick did rob and kill Uncle Jeff, that money won't last him long and he'll be looking for more. He'll have gotten away with one killing, and another one or two or three, even, wouldn't likely bother him none. So none of us would be safe around here. Not me nor any of my neighbors. Now I don't believe in tellin' stories on a man, Marshal, but when it comes to something like this . . . anyhow, this Nick Root, he's more like some kind o' swamp critter than a man, I reckon."

"Thanks again, Mr. Appleyard. I'd better be ridin' back to Dodge pronto and try to catch up with Nick. If he is the killer and too much talk gets around about him flashing a lot of money, he's likely to get scared and run out. Let you know what happens. My regards to your missus."

"Glad to help, Marshal."

As the conversation ended, young Richie Appleyard, who had been inching closer and closer to his father and the Marshal, scuttled furiously back to his pony, as his father looked around.

"You young imp!" Appleyard shouted. "You'd better get back there. I hope that four-footed demon throws you good next time, to punish you for listenin' in on other people's conversations. I've taught you better manners than that, you whippersnapper. . . ."

Appleyard's tirade at his son was still going on as Marshal Dillon rode away from the homestead, grinning to himself, despite the serious matters that were on his mind.

9 *Hideaway Shack*

Before he headed back to Dodge, Marshal Dillon decided that since it wasn't too much out of his way, it would be a good idea to stop at Nick Root's shack, on the off-chance that the man might have decided to go home to rest before returning to the city again tonight. At the same time, Dillon thought it would be a good idea to look around Root's place. If Root were the killer, the chances were that he wouldn't take all that money into Dodge with him. He might have some of it hidden around his shack.

If Dillon could find that money hidden on Root's property, it would be strong evidence of the man's guilt.

Nick Root's home was a tarpaper-covered, ramshackle shed thrown up hastily by fishermen as a shelter during bad weather, some years before.

It was located in a small clearing, near the edge of a lazy,

165

murky backwater stream. The land all around it was treacherous bog, once you got off the filled-in narrow path that led down to the water's edge from higher ground.

The stench of dead fish and swamp muck was strong about the place.

At one side of the shack was a waist-high pile of broken jars and bottles and other trash. Spread out across some nearby shrubbery to dry, some time ago judging by their stiffened condition, was a pair of patched and threadbare Levi's. A pair of broken-over and mud-daubed work shoes stood next to the doorway of the place.

Nailed to the front door of the shack, which was held shut by an ancient and rusty padlock, was a crudely lettered sign that said:

KEPE AWAY!

SNUPERS WIL

BE SHOT ON

SITE!!!

Dillon approached cautiously, mindful of the two huge and vicious, half-starved mongrel dogs that Root kept around the place. He wondered why the dogs weren't already running at him, yelping and snarling. Then, as he rode into what passed as the yard, he saw why.

Both dogs lay sprawled out, munching lazily at the little that remained of a woodchuck they had caught and killed. Their bellies were already bulging with all they had gorged themselves on. They cocked sleepy red-rimmed eyes toward Dillon as he rode up and one of them growled half-heartedly. The other one merely paused in his eating for a moment to inspect Dillon curiously, then went back to his meal.

As Dillon dismounted, he spoke in a low, kindly voice to the dogs and they both gave brief wags of their ragged tails, convinced now that he wasn't going to try to share their meal.

The rusty lock on Root's door snapped open with one good smash of the bottom of Dillon's boot against it.

The Marshal didn't like to break into somebody's home like this, even such a sorry excuse for a home as this one was. But he told himself that under the circumstances he had no choice. Then, too, when he caught up to Root, he would tell the man what he had done and even buy him a new lock.

When Dillon shoved the door open with his foot, he hesitated for a moment before venturing inside. The place, with no windows in it and the only ventilation coming from cracks between boards, reeked for lack of fresh air. Making a face, Dillon wondered if Nick Root had had sense enough to buy himself a rain-water bath in town before putting on his newly bought clothes.

When Dillon shoved the door open, the inside of the shack seemed pitch black. After waiting a few moments, though, Dillon's eyes became accustomed to the dimness inside. Then, just as he was about to enter, he sucked in a breath of surprise. He said a small prayer of thanks that he had waited before stumbling blindly into the shed.

Set on the floor just inside the door, opened and waiting for some unwary foot to step down between its great, rusty, jagged-edged jaws, was a bear trap.

"Phew!" Dillon wiped perspiration from his upper lip. "I'll bet Nick Root has just been hopin' somebody would blunder into that thing some day. A man who could set something like that for another human being to get caught in is capable of anything."

He reached out and picked up an old hoe handle standing next to the door. With it he poked gingerly at the bear trap. Almost at the first touch, the thing clanked shut with such force that it leaped a foot into the air.

"That would snap the bone in a man's leg like a tooth-pick," Dillon told himself.

He kicked the now harmless trap to one side and entered the shack, feeling his way cautiously through the dimness, fearful of other possible traps. After a moment his fingers touched the edge of a roughly hewn table. They moved along the top until they contacted an old cracked and dusty hurricane lamp. Dillon lit it and looked about the interior of the shack.

Some crudely tanned animal skins were stretched out on frames on two of the walls. The only bed was a pile of old and half-rotten comforters lumped together at one side of the room on the floor.

A spider scuttled under the table. In one corner of the room a rat squealed and squeezed its way out under a wall in rustling terror. Dillon shivered in spite of himself at the aura of dirt and evil that seemed to hang over the place.

Looking around, he saw that as poorly as the place was furnished, there wasn't anything that faintly resembled a good hiding place for money. He walked over to the bedding on the floor and kicked it to one side. The ground under it had not been disturbed recently. Nor had the rest of the dirt floor inside the shack.

Dillon realized then that if Nick Root had the money and had hidden part of it, he probably would have done so outside somewhere—in some hollow tree or stump that he knew about. There were so many possible hiding places for something like that outside, that it was useless for Dillon even to think about it.

He was just about to start for the door, was set to blow out the lamp, when he saw a small, round object shining on the floor. Swiftly he moved toward it, bent and picked it up. On closer examination in the light of the lamp, he saw that it was a shiny piece of brass saddle-trapping.

At the same moment, Dillon remembered that out in the yard he had noticed the fresh imprint of hoofs. He knew that Nick Root didn't own a horse. Then who had been here?

Fear rippled up Marshal Dillon's backbone for an instant as he realized that this would be an ideal place for the ex-convict, Huggins, to hide out. Huggins might even be a friend of Nick Root's. Perhaps the two of them had been in on the robbery and murder together! If that were true, Dillon realized, it was possible that Huggins had heard him approaching, might even now be waiting outside to shoot him from ambush as he stepped out the door.

If so, Marshal Dillon knew he was caught in a deadly trap. There was no other exit from the shack.

A moment later he blew out the lamp and edged as quietly as possible toward the door. When he reached it, he took off his Stetson and cautiously pushed it out the edge of the doorway at head height. He figured that Huggins was probably too shrewd a man to be taken in by such an old trick, but there wasn't much else to be tried. He had nothing to lose.

Nothing happened. There was no shot from the dense swampland underbrush all around the edge of the clearing.

Dillon waited a moment more, then bent over low and hurtled through the door, hitting the ground as soon as possible and rolling over and over, hunched up to make himself as small and difficult a target as possible.

He rolled to the edge of the clearing and still there was no shot. There was no sound at all, except the twittering of irate birds in the shrubbery and the rustling of dried leaves as a highly indignant chipmunk ran chittering away.

Dillon breathed a sigh of relief, feeling a little foolish now, and got to his feet. He dusted himself off and walked over to where he had tethered his horse to a small tree. He forked the saddle and walked his mount carefully up the narrow gravel trail toward higher ground. There he turned the horse toward the trail that led back to Dodge.

The sun was beginning to set, and in another half hour or so darkness would shut down tightly over the country, bringing with it refreshing relief from the brutal summer sun.

10   *Time Grows Short*

Lights were beginning to glow from the windows of shops and houses in Dodge City, when Marshal Matt Dillon rode in that evening. With the dusk a softness seemed to have settled on this harsh frontier town. The false fronts of some of the buildings no longer looked sun-scorched and ugly. Rising against the purple night sky, they looked to Matt Dillon for a moment almost pretty, like the fronts of toy buildings in a toy town.

But the illusion didn't last long. He remembered some of the trouble that happened behind those same false fronts.

Front Street—in fact, the whole of Dodge—was always quiet at this time of evening. The town seemed peaceful. It was hard to realize, riding along the almost deserted, twilight-touched street, that in a few hours almost any kind of violence could, and probably would, happen along those same streets. Right now, most folks were taking a brief rest, cleaning up after a day's work, or eating their dinner. Later they would stream out onto the streets. A bunch of trail hands would come whooping and roaring in from their camp outside of Dodge, ready to paint the town. The wheels would begin to spin in the gambling casinos. There would be the soft shuffling of playing cards in clever, professional hands.

Sooner or later, a fight would break out somewhere. Somebody would be hurt, perhaps killed.

Ordinarily all of these things would come under the heading of work for Marshal Matt Dillon. He would be expected to restrain the Texas trail hands and somehow keep them from breaking up the town, without spoiling any of their fun. He would have to stop the fight before flaring tempers turned it into a mob brawl.

But tonight, Dillon knew, most of these routine tasks would have to be handed over to his deputy, Chester Good. Dillon hoped that if Doc Adams wasn't busy, he would watch the jail for them while Chester made the rounds of the town, trying to keep order. Dillon would be busy trying to pin down the murderer of a kind old man who had never had an enemy in the world.

Dillon rode to the hitching rail in front of the jailhouse and dismounted. Around the edges of a drawn shade, light from a lamp shone faintly. Dillon tried the door and found it locked.

"Open up," he said. "Hurry it, Chester. We've got things to do."

Doc Adams' gruff old voice answered through the door, "Hold your horses, and it isn't Chester in here, so stop orderin' people around so—so officiously, Matt Dillon."

The door was unbolted and Dillon stepped inside.

"What are you doin' here, Doc? Where's Chester?"

"The boy, Tommy Gant, wanted Chester to come around and see him for a while. Wanted to show Chester some tricks or something he's learned from those silly mail-order pamphlets. So I've been spellin' Chester a bit."

"Good, Doc. I was hopin' you'd take over here this evenin' while Chester makes the rounds for me. I've got some business down the other side of the Deadline."

The Deadline, of course, was a mythical boundary along the railroad tracks, dividing Dodge into two business sections. In previous days, during the regime of Wyatt Earp and others, no one was supposed to carry guns past the Deadline into the legitimate and main business section of the town. Below the Deadline was the section for whooping-it-up, and nobody bothered much what happened down there. That section of the town hadn't changed much.

"Well, I'll be switched!" Doc said, clucking his tongue and pretending to be disgusted. "First you stay out loafin' all afternoon and now you want other people to do your jobs for you while you go high-tailin' it around the dead-falls down on Texas Street."

Dillon refused to be drawn into the usual good-natured bantering this evening. His face beginning to look over-tired, he busied himself at his desk, looking through some papers.

"I see there still isn't any answer to that telegram I sent to the territorial prison about the personal articles checked out by Gant and Huggins when they were released."

He left the desk and walked over to the cell that held Jan Gant. The big, rawboned homesteader was sitting on the edge of his bunk, his great hands resting on his knees, the fingers laced tightly together. He looked up at Dillon and tried to work up a smile; it came out nothing more than a flickering of his facial muscles.

"Marshal, you have any luck?" Gant asked. His voice sounded as though his throat were raw. "You turn up anything on Huggins—or anybody?"

Dillon leaned against the bars, feeling the coolness of the steel against his face. "I'm afraid not much, Gant. I've got a new lead that might turn into something, but then might not. . . . Jan, did you ever hear Huggins mention a man named Nick Root? He's new in this section since you went away."

Gant thought about it, pushing his fingers up into the long, tangled sideburns at his temples. "No. The name doesn't sound familiar, at all."

"Ah!" Doc said. "I've been just waitin' to hear that mean and ornery critter, that calls itself a man, has got himself into big trouble. You know what that sidewinder did, Matt? Set out chunks of poisoned dough along that creek where he lives, to get rid of water birds that were disturbing his fishing. And knowin' blamed well that some of the kids who live in that river bottom section—some of them real little ones—often go down to that shallow creek to catch crayfish."

"And one of them got some of the poisoned dough. Is that what happened, Doc?" Dillon asked.

"Yup." For a moment Doc looked as though he were about to cry. "One of those little Nichols girls, who never

look like they get enough to eat, anyhow, got it. Matt, that child came this close to dyin'!" Doc held up his thumb and forefinger, indicating a hairbreadth of space.

"When I went down to try to talk that skunk into bein' careful where he sets that stuff out, and explained what happened, you know what he did, Matt?"

"I can imagine."

"He just laughed in my face like some idiotic jungle hyena, that's what he did. Then pointed an old blunderbuss of a shotgun right at my middle and gave me till the count of three to get off his property. He was just dyin' to shoot me and then claim he did it because I was trespassin'. I could see that in those mad eyes of his. Well, sir, I was in such a hurry to get away from that blunderbuss, I tripped over a root and almost broke my dratted neck. That made Root laugh more like a hyena than ever. Matt, sometimes I wonder why men like that are even created."

"I can just see that, Doc," Dillon told him. "I mean, you with your coattails flyin', in the face of that cannon of Root's."

Then Dillon told Doc Adams and Gant what he had heard about Nick Root suddenly flashing a lot of big money down below the Deadline.

When he had finished, Jan Gant grasped the bars tightly. His face was screwed up with emotion and he was having trouble holding back tears.

"Marshal," he begged, "you've got to get this Nick Root or Huggins, or whoever the real killer is, soon. It can't be too soon, Marshal. For my wife's sake, if not mine."

"What do you mean, Gant? Is your wife any worse?"

"Doc won't tell me any of the details, but I *know*, Marshal. I know how my wife is, what something like this will do to her, on top of her bein' so weak and all. It'll kill her, Marshal, if I'm not cleared soon."

Dillon turned to Doc Adams. "How about that?"

Doc shrugged and looked away. "It's hard to say, Matt. Mrs. Gant perked up a little when Tommy stayed with her. He cheered her a mite. But then she seemed to get more depressed. She can't eat and she's gettin' weaker by the hour. I'll be frank with you, Matt, she *has* taken this thing hard. Nothin' much is goin' to help, outside of her husband being set free."

"That lynch mob talk hasn't helped her any either," Gant said. "You couldn't for the life of you make her believe that bunch won't bust in here and drag me out and hang me, if I stay in here much longer."

"Has Galloway and that bunch been around here while I was gone, Gant?" Dillon asked sharply.

"I don't know who they were," Gant said. "Sounded like quite a mob of them out there on the street. They pelted rocks at the door. They kept hollering in a sort of chant, 'Hang the Killer! Hang the Killer!'"

Dillon looked at Doc. "How in the world did Mrs. Gant hear about that? You'd think people would have more sense than to tell a frightened, sick woman about something like that."

"She heard somebody passing along the hall of the rooming house, outside her door, and they were talking about it. Matt, I tried to tell her it was all just talk but she wouldn't believe me. She got hysterical and finally fainted."

"I just hope it *is* all talk," Dillon said. "Doc, I've got to go after Nick Root now. When Chester comes back, tell him to make the rounds for me."

He waved toward the door of Gant's cell. "Keep your chin up, mister. Maybe this'll be it. If Root's our man, you'll be out of here before morning."

Outside, Dillon saw that the full dark of a moonless night had come down over the city. Long shadows, cast by the flickering glow from a pine knot torch in front of one of the saloons, lay crookedly across Front Street, as Dillon walked away from the jailhouse.

A moment later, from the street in front of the Long Branch, where Dillon could see a mob of people had gathered, there was a cheer. He heard the bull-like voice of Mike Galloway roaring something to the crowd.

The Marshal lengthened his stride. He reached down and automatically loosened his six-gun in its holster. He heard the mob roar its approval of something else Galloway shouted at them, and he walked even faster.

Closer now, Dillon saw that the group gathered in the street in front of the Long Branch was much larger than the gang that had gathered in front of the jailhouse, earlier today, waiting for Jan Gant to be brought in. There were close to fifty or sixty people in this group. A few of them were women.

Dillon knew that wasn't good. Any mob is hard to control, but a mob with even a few women members is that much more difficult to handle. They make the men in the crowd more daring, bolder, more inclined to show off their defiance of law and order.

As Dillon approached, a man stationed at the outer edge of the throng, obviously to watch out for him, made a sign with his waving arms to Mike Galloway, who was standing on a packing crate.

Almost instantly, Galloway stopped his ranting and looked toward Dillon. So did the mob. Several men, feeling secure in the density of the crowd around them, made jeering remarks about the Marshal. Dillon ignored these. He stood at the outer edge of the crowd and looked across their heads toward Galloway, who was now grinning broadly.

"Evenin', Marshal," Galloway called. "Ain't you wanted elsewhere? I hear there's a couple of old ladies having a wicked hair-pulling contest in a house over on Kansas Street."

The throng whooped with laughter.

"Galloway," Dillon said, "I suppose you know there's a law against inciting a street mob to violence. If you don't want to try one of our empty cells, I'd advise you to tell this bunch to break up and go about their business."

"Violence, Marshal?" Galloway said with a pretense of extreme innocence. "We wouldn't know what you're talking about, would we, ladies and gentlemen? This happens to be an extremely peaceful gathering, Marshal."

Impatiently, Dillon told him, "I didn't come down here

to crack jokes with you, Galloway. You're trying to form a lynch mob to get Jan Gant out of jail and hang him. There's talk of it all over town. But I'm telling you right now that you won't ever do it. Because I'll personally see to it, Galloway, that no matter what happens to me, you'll die in the attempt! Think about that."

"Why, I don't see any lynch mob, Marshal," Galloway continued, appearing undisturbed by the Marshal's serious threat. "And you never did say what violence you're talking about."

"Galloway, half the people in this crowd are carrying ax handles, hoe handles, and other kinds of clubs. What are they planning to use them for, if not violence of some sort?"

"Why, I wouldn't know, Marshal. Maybe they're just carrying them home. Is there a law against carrying such articles, Marshal?"

"If they're to be used as weapons, there is."

"But you can't prove that, Marshal. Or do you claim to be able to read people's minds?"

"I can read yours, Galloway, and it isn't very good reading. I told you, before—break up this lynch mob."

Galloway was getting bored with being pleasant in a nasty sort of way. His mouth turned down at the corners, he leaned forward. His face grew red with anger.

"And I'm telling you that you can't prove it's a lynch mob, Marshal. Until you can do that, leave us alone. As far as you're concerned this is just a group of Dodge City citizens, holding a public political demonstration. But not such a public one that we want the Marshal joining with us. Get about your job, Marshal, and leave us alone."

Then Galloway stood there silently, with his stout, heavily muscled arms folded across his chest. Dillon realized that he wasn't going to work on the crowd again until the Marshal was out of hearing range. And what Galloway had said was true. As long as the group was reasonably orderly and Dillon couldn't prove that they were a potential lynch mob, there wasn't anything he could do about them.

"All right, Galloway, I'm leaving now," Dillon told him finally. "But every one of you in this crowd listen to me. No matter how convincing Mike Galloway may sound, don't let him talk you into trying to storm the jailhouse. There's still a large shadow of doubt about Jan Gant's guilt. Right now I'm on my way to check a lead that may turn up the man who is undeniably the killer."

A vast silence greeted that announcement. Then Mike Galloway burst into laughter, briefly. "You mean you're after Huggins, Gant's friend?" Galloway asked.

"I didn't say it was Huggins."

"Oh, come now, Marshal! It's got to be either Gant or Huggins—or more likely both. I'll tell you what, Marshal, I'll make a deal with you. You bring in this coyote Huggins and stick him in jail along with his friend Gant, and I promise you there won't be any more trouble. I swear it."

"There won't be any trouble anyhow, Galloway. I don't have to make deals with you to keep this town peaceable."

Then Dillon addressed the others: "You men of Dodge know I always aim to see justice done. Why don't you stop being so hasty, letting a rabble-rouser like Galloway try to talk you into doing something you may all be sorry about later? Just think how you'd feel if you did what Galloway wants you to do and then learned that you'd hung the wrong man! Could any of you live with your conscience after that? Give me a little more time, men, and we'll see that the right man is tried and punished pronto for this crime."

Dillon turned then, and walked down the street toward the Deadline. When a momentary silence followed, he knew that he had gotten through to the better instincts of some of the members of the mob, at least for the time being. But then some of the others started jeering and cat-calling after him and he knew, too, that it would be just a matter of time before the mob, under Galloway's hate-inspired goading, would reach a point where nothing could stop them.

He figured he had a couple of hours at the most before the mob was completely won over. Eventually Galloway, who was much admired by the kind of men who would form the solid core of a hate-mad lynch mob, would win out. Unless, of course, Dillon could make another arrest, based on good, solid evidence.

11   *Below the Deadline*

In the main section of Dodge City only a few people resented Marshal Matt Dillon and refused to co-operate with him. Most of the citizens were happy and proud to have such a loyal, honest, tough peace officer serving them.

The part of town below the Deadline was different. Here all the backwash of society, the misfits, people who refused to live by the rules because the rules sometimes interfered with their own selfish pleasures, who for one reason or another couldn't seem to get along in the world of decent, respectable people—here was their living quarters and playground.

Below the Deadline almost everybody resented Matt Dillon and refused to co-operate. They felt the same way about any representative of the law but especially so toward an officer of Dillon's fame. Yet at the same time they held

a sort of sullen respect for the power and quickness of his
fists, for the swiftness of his draw. While they didn't go out
of their way to help him, neither did they dare go to great
lengths to obstruct him.

The first place Dillon visited, searching for Nick Root,
was a gambling casino called The Blue Devil. It was run
by a man called Mr. Big. Few people knew his real name.
He ruled as unofficial mayor of the section of town below
the Deadline.

Entering The Blue Devil, Dillon made his way through
the big, noisy, smoke-filled room, toward a door at the back,
upon which was crudely printed the word *Office*.

The man called Mr. Big was sitting at a huge, roll-top
desk, leafing through an ancient ledger filled with figures
and notations. He swung around on his chair when Dillon
entered.

Mr. Big lived up to his name. He was one of the largest
men Matt Dillon had ever met. He weighed well over three
hundred pounds. His neck was so fat that it didn't seem
like a neck at all but part of his great sloping, beefy shoulders that filled an outsized silk shirt. The arm bands that
held up the sleeves of the shirt had to be especially made for
him, to fit around the thickness of his arms. Mr. Big had,

surprisingly enough, extra-small features that seemed altogether lost in the fat of his face. His mouth looked like a tiny, pink rosebud pushed into all that flesh. His nose resembled a too-small dab of putty that had been stuck on as an afterthought. His eyes were like small, shiny black buttons; his head was completely bald.

There was little pretense of politeness below the Dead-line. Ignoring the usual greetings, Mr. Big just stared hard at Dillon with his small eyes and said in a voice surprisingly high for such a big man, "What is it, Marshal?"

Dillon played the game their way, down here, as much as possible. He came just as quickly to the point. "I'm look-ing for a man named Nick Root. Is he still down in your part of town?"

"Have you looked?"

"I don't want to waste a lot of time looking for him if he's not still here. If he's still here, you know about it. Do you want me barging through a lot of places, making people nervous and spoiling business, if it isn't necessary?"

"No," Mr. Big said.

He took a brown-paper cigarette from an ebony box on the desk and fitted it carefully into his tiny kewpie-bowed mouth. He lit it and puffed out smoke and then, rolling

the cigarette slowly between his sausage-sized fingers, he said, "He's at Red Bricker's place."

Dillon ducked his head. "Thanks," he said and turned to leave Mr. Big's office.

"Marshal," Mr. Big said.

Dillon paused, turning around, "Yes?"

"You won't take Root easy. He's got too much money and been havin' too much fun to want to bother with the law. He'll give you a hard time."

"I know. Thanks for the warning, though."

"Don't kill him if you can help it," Mr. Big said. "Killings down here are contagious. One starts and there'll be a lot more."

"I won't kill him if I can help it. I want Root alive."

Mr. Big said, "I hope that's the way you get him." He turned around and went back to work adding up the columns of figures in his ledger.

Dillon left the office, left The Blue Devil. The place owned by Red Bricker was only a few doors down the street. It was similar to the gambling place Dillon had just left. Although smaller, it was smokier and noisier.

When Dillon walked into the place, some of the noise lessened. Nobody in the place looked directly at him. If they watched him at all, it was from the corner of an eye.

For a few moments Dillon couldn't see much in the dimly lit, smoke-filled room. Then, as his eyes became more accustomed to the semi-gloom, he looked around at the gambling tables. He saw no sign of Nick Root. He glanced along the bar. Half a dozen men were standing there, but none of them was Root. Dillon walked over to the bar.

The bartender was a skinny little man with black, slicked-down hair that made a sharp widow's peak at the top of his high forehead. He had a sallow complexion and a sour, unhappy expression on his thin face. As Dillon stood at the bar, the barkeeper reached for a bottle. Matt held up his hand.

"No, thanks," he said. "Is a man named Nick Root here?"

The bartender looked at him blankly. After a moment he said, "I don't know my customers by name."

"I was told he was here. Mr. Big told me."

The bartender shrugged his bony shoulders. He stuck a celluloid toothpick between his teeth and spoke around it. "Mebbe he is. Mebbe he isn't. I wouldn't know."

Dillon looked toward a stairway at the back of the place. "Is he upstairs?"

As if in answer, Dillon, still looking toward the stairs,

saw a man come through a door at the top and start down the stairs. As he did so, his eyes swept the room below until they found Matt Dillon. Then his eyes stayed right on Dillon's.

Nick Root was about thirty years old, a compactly built man who would have been good looking, except for the bitter, cruel twist to his thin slash of mouth and the cold emptiness of his very pale blue eyes. There seemed to be no human expression at all in those eyes. Root's hair was thick and curly and black and gleaming with hair oil. He was wearing nothing but black. His black shirt, black whip-cord riding breeches, and gleaming black boots were cheaply made but obviously new.

Nick Root wore no gun rig, but Dillon had heard once that he carried a needle-pointed, razor-sharp knife in a scabbard that hung down the back of his neck, under his shirt.

As Root reached the bottom of the stairs, he walked with an easy-moving, catlike grace, away from the bar, toward a table in a dark corner of the room. When his back was turned to Dillon, the Marshal noticed a slight movement of Root's right arm.

Dillon left the bar and walked over to Root's table. The

man was sitting there now, his hands out of sight under the table, his back to a wall. Dillon reached the table and pulled out a chair. He turned it around toward him and sat down, straddling the chair, his arms resting on the top of its back.

Up close, Dillon saw that the only signs of Root's all-day carousing below the Deadline were a redness around the rims of his eyes and a twitch at one corner of his mouth.

"You're Nick Root, aren't you?" Dillon asked.

Root formed a smile that made him look like a snarling animal. He had small, sharp-looking teeth. The skin around his eyes wrinkled like parchment, with that grin.

"Am I?" Root said.

"You'd better answer my questions straight out, Root. I didn't look you up to play games."

"Didn't you?" The senseless grin stayed on Root's face as though it were frozen there. His vacant-looking pale blue eyes held Dillon's in an unblinking stare.

"I hear you've been throwing a lot of money around down here all day, Root," Dillon said. "Even got yourself some new clothes. Where did the money come from?"

"Not where you think. Let's say I earned the money."

"How?"

Root shrugged. "There are ways."

"Such as killing and robbing an old man like Jeff Foster?"

The grin vanished from Root's face. His mouth pursed up tightly. He leaned forward against the table. "You aren't going to pin that on me. I haven't killed anybody. You hear?" His voice rose shrilly.

"Then where did the money come from?"

"I won it, Marshal. Gambling."

Dillon stood up and swung his chair back under the table. "All right. That should be easy enough to check. Get up, Root. You're coming with me. You're going to take me to the place where you won that money."

"If I don't?" Root's right arm moved slightly but his hands still remained hidden under the table.

"Nick Root, you listen to me," Dillon said, then. "I've heard a lot about you—none of it any good. If you want to play it rough, that's fine with me. Now, you're going to do one of two things: either prove to me where you suddenly got a lot of money, or come along for questioning about the murder of Uncle Jeff Foster."

Root's thin lips drew back across his small teeth, but there was no resemblance to a grin in the expression this time. He said, "I can't tell you where I got that hundred dollars, Marshal. But I can't let you jail me for Foster's murder, either. You'd better leave me alone, Marshal."

"A hundred dollars?" Dillon asked. "You sure there isn't more than that?"

"A hundred goes a long way down here below the Deadline, Marshal. That's all I had and most of it's gone."

"You still haven't told me where you got it, Root. If you can't account for it any other way, I'll have to assume it was part of the money stolen from Jeff Foster. Now talk quick, Root, or get up from there and come with me."

Nick Root shook his head slowly, from side to side.

"Root, there's a man in jail technically charged with Foster's murder, because of certain evidence. But there's a better than even chance that he's innocent. There's also a lynch mob formed that wants Jan Gant's neck in a rope and before very long they could get out of hand. I haven't got time to fool with you, Root. Get up from that table."

"I could kill you right this minute, Marshal," Root said. "Nobody in this place would say they saw it. I'd get plumb away with it. You get out of here and leave me alone, Marshal, or I might just do that."

Dillon knew, then, what he had only suspected before. Nick Root had been carrying a gun tucked in his belt, under his shirt. He had taken it out while walking toward the table. Now he was probably holding that gun, cocked and ready to fire, out of sight under the table.

If Dillon had to kill Root to defend himself, he might never be able to get proof that Nick Root was the killer. Somehow he had to take the man alive.

"I don't think you're goin' to do any killing tonight, Root," Dillon said.

Swiftly, the Marshal brought his knee up under the edge of the table, ramming it over backward and partially pinning Nick Root between the table and the wall. Root made a squealing noise of alarm and tried to wriggle free. He managed to get his right hand out from under the table. It held a tiny, palm-sized weapon called a derringer. A derringer was just as deadly up close as a larger gun.

A fraction of a second before the gun fired, Dillon grabbed Root's arm, thrusting it upward. The bullet whistled just over the Marshal's head. He twisted Root's arm and the derringer fell to the floor. At the same time Root, wiry and quick, writhed free and got out from behind the table. As Dillon lunged to grab him, Root's hand darted behind his neck and came up holding a thin, gleaming, deadly, thin-bladed knife.

Just as Root thrust the knife in a vicious, arcing strike, Dillon, moving with lightninglike speed for such a big man, twisted to one side and then moved in close before Root could strike again. He got Root's right arm in both hands and bent it until Root cried out.

"Drop the knife, Root!" Dillon ordered. "I don't want to break your arm but I can't let you cut me up with that pig-sticker, either."

The knife clattered to the floor. Still, Dillon didn't release Root's arm. "All right, Root, now tell me where you got the money. I want the truth."

All fight suddenly was gone out of Nick Root. His face twisted and, half sobbing, he blurted, "I'll tell you, Marshal! I'll tell you the truth and I can prove it, but don't break my arm."

Dillon released his hold. Root stood there, rubbing his arm, looking down at the floor. He was trembling violently.

"I didn't want to tell you, Marshal, because I thought you wouldn't believe me. You'd think I'd stolen the horse and killed the man who owned it."

"What horse are you talking about, Root?"

"The one I found grazing near my place. There was nobody around and there was blood all over the saddle, Marshal, so I figured it out that the man who'd owned the horse had been shot and had fallen off."

"When was this?"

"Early this morning, just before dawn."

"All right. Go on."

"Well, Marshal, I hitched the horse outside my place. When several hours went by, I figured the man who owned it was probably dead and wasn't coming around looking for it. So I cleaned the blood from the saddle and brought the horse into town. I sold the horse and saddle trappings to a small livery on Bleek Street, a place where they don't ask too many questions."

"All right, Root," Dillon said. "Let's go to that livery and check your story. I want to take a look at that horse too."

Together, they left Red Bricker's place.

12   *"Hang Jan Gant!"*

The livery where Nick Root claimed to have sold the horse was only a few blocks from Bricker's place. It was a sleazy-looking, rundown stable owned by a man named Max Silver, a dried-up little old man who always had a frowning, worried look on his leathery face.

When Dillon and Root entered the livery, Max Silver was mending the torn top of an old secondhand buggy. In nearby stalls, several horses whinnied. The moment Silver saw Dillon and Root, he walked swiftly toward them, wringing his hands.

"Marshal," he said before the other could speak, "if the horse this man sold me was stolen, I didn't know it. I'm not responsible. He swore to me that it wasn't. I even made him sign a paper to that effect. I don't want any trouble with the law, Marshal."

"I see. Then he is telling the truth. You did buy a horse from him. How much did you pay for it?"

"One hundred dollars, Marshal. I got a good buy for the money, so you can't blame me for taking it. If the horse was stolen, I'll be glad to turn it over to its rightful owner, if he'll refund the money. Horse and trappings are worth considerable more than that, Marshal."

Marshal Dillon's heart had sunk when he learned that Nick Root had been telling the truth. For a while he had been sure the man was lying, that he wouldn't be able to explain where he had gotten the money, and that it was really some of the cash stolen from Jeff Foster. Now that theory was out. Nick Root could no longer even be considered a suspect.

That left Dillon with Jan Gant still the only one.

Then Dillon thought of something. He said to Silver, "I want to see this horse."

"Sure, Marshal," Silver said eagerly. "Right this way." He picked up a lantern and led Dillon to one of the stalls.

"Would you be good enough to bring him out here into the light?" Dillon asked.

A moment later Silver led the horse out of the stall. It was a black gelding and its only unusual marking was a small blaze on its forehead, shaped roughly like a four-leaf clover.

"All right," Dillon said. "I think I might know who owned this horse. I'll find out in a little while."

"Will—will he want the horse back?" Silver asked.

"Not if it's who I think it is," Dillon answered. "That man's probably dead."

"What about me, Marshal?" Nick Root asked. "It was like I said, wasn't it? I didn't steal the horse. I found him running loose, like I said."

Dillon had a pretty strong idea that the black horse had belonged to Huggins. It was possible that Huggins had been the one who robbed and killed Uncle Jeff Foster. For a moment he considered the possibility that Nick Root might, in turn, have murdered the ex-convict.

Then he had to dismiss the idea. If that had happened, Root wouldn't have dared bring the horse into town where somebody might identify it as Huggins'. He would be a fool to do that. Nor would he then have had to sell the horse to get money. That theory was out, Dillon was sure.

He turned to Nick Root. "When you found that horse, Root, you should have turned him over to me. If nobody claimed him within a reasonable time, then the horse would have been legally yours. As it stands, I've got a charge against you for selling property that wasn't legally your own."

"Marshal, I don't want to go to jail," Root whimpered. "I—I'll get a job and earn enough money to pay the hundred back to Silver. Wouldn't that help, Marshal?"

"It might, if you could hold a job long enough to earn a hundred dollars. From what people think of you, you probably couldn't even get a job. But I'll tell you what I'm going to do. You go on home, Root. If I ever hear one complaint about you—mind you—or if any more foodstuff is stolen from any of the homesteads out your way, I'll haul you in, Root. And I'll press charges on this. You understand?"

"Yes, Marshal. I sure do. . . . Then I—I can go now?"

Dillon nodded. He watched Nick Root scurry for the door. Then he turned to Silver.

"I'd advise you to be a little more careful about the people you buy horseflesh from."

"I—it doesn't pay to ask too many questions of people down in this end of town, Marshal. A man can get in trouble that way."

"He can get into trouble by buying stolen property too.

Bear that in mind, Mr. Silver."

"Yes, sir, Marshal," Silver said, frowning worriedly.

Dillon headed for the door of the livery.

A little later, back on Front Street, the Marshal saw that Galloway's mob had moved from in front of the Long Branch, up the street, and were now congregated in front of the jail building. As Dillon moved toward them, he heard the crowd shouting, "We want Gant! We want Gant! We want Jan Gant!"

Then someone in the crowd saw Dillon and hollered, "Here he comes! Here comes the Marshal now! Tell him what we want, Galloway, and no more shilly-shallyin'!"

When Dillon reached the jailhouse, he stopped and faced the crowd blocking his way. He saw that Galloway had talked most of them into a frenzy. Most of the men looked wild-eyed and dangerous in the flickering red glow of the pine knot torches some of them carried. Most of them, too, Dillon could see, had been bolstering their courage with frequent trips to the saloons, which wouldn't make them any easier to reason with.

A man in the back of the crowd yelled, "Marshal, we've waited long enough. We're goin' to hang Jan Gant for killin' ol' Jeff Foster. Either you turn him over to us or

we'll go in and take him. One way or the other, we got to
do that!"

Mike Galloway stood in the front of the crowd, grinning
at Dillon. "You heard them, Marshal," he said. "What are
you going to do about it?"

"Nothing," Dillon told him. "I don't answer to mob
rule. I thought this was a peaceful crowd, Galloway. What
made you decide to come right out into the open and say
what you're really up to?"

"We thought we'd give you some time, Marshal, to find
another suspect—if there was one," Galloway told him.
"You see, we gave you the benefit of the doubt, Marshal,
figuring that you honestly weren't sure Gant was guilty.
But you haven't been able to find anybody else who could
have killed Foster, have you?"

"I haven't completed the investigation yet," Dillon answered.

"How long's it goin' to take you?"

"That's my business."

"We're makin' it ours, too, Marshal." He turned to the
crowd. "Aren't we, friends?"

The mob shouted its approval.

"You see, Marshal," Galloway said, "my friends are

gettin' impatient. Jeff Foster was robbed and murdered some time last night. You've had all day to find another suspect and it looks as though you aren't goin' to find one. The way we see it, there's enough evidence against Gant to call for his hanging. Me and my friends here want to see justice done—and fast, Marshal. So, why don't you go along with what the citizens of the town want, and turn your prisoner over to us?"

"So you can string him up somewhere without even a fair trial? You aren't going to do that, Galloway."

"We'll give him a trial," a man next to Galloway said. "We'll hold a kangaroo court right here on the street. We'll appoint a judge and jury right from this crowd."

"That's right, Marshal. A regular court might be too easy on Gant, the way they were last time he killed a man."

From the back of the crowd, then, someone shouted, "There's been enough talk. Now let's *do* somethin'! If the Marshal won't turn his prisoner over to us and see justice done, let's grab the Marshal and hold him prisoner until Chester brings out Gant!"

This announcement was greeted with wild cheers from the crowd. Some of those in the back began to push forward impatiently.

Marshal Dillon backed up a step. His hand dropped to his gun butt. He shifted his feet and his body leaned forward a little in his gun-fighting stance.

"Galloway, you listen to me," he said. "If this crowd makes one more move toward me, I'll shoot you as their leader."

There was silence for a moment and then somebody said, "You goin' to let him bluff you like that, Galloway?"

"Galloway knows I don't bluff," Dillon said.

"This crowd would swarm all over you and tear you apart with their bare hands, Marshal," Galloway said, "if you shot me."

"Maybe so. But that wouldn't help you much, would it, Galloway? You'd still be dead." Dillon waited a moment for that to sink in, then he went on, "Now break a path for me through this crowd. I'm going into my office."

He moved toward them, walking slowly, deliberately. He said, "Just remember—the first man who tries to lay a hand on me will die!"

Slowly, mumbling and grumbling and muttering, the crowd opened up before Matt Dillon. They formed a narrow lane between them. Dillon walked silently on through them. Then he moved up to the jailhouse office door. As he was unlocking it, he heard Mike Galloway's voice.

"All right, Marshal! We've let you overrule us for the last time. We'll give you one more hour. *One hour!* Do you hear that? In exactly one hour from now, either you bring Jan Gant out here to us, or we come in and get him. . . . Is that right, friends?"

The mob roared its approval. There was a fierce ringing to the sound that told Dillon that they had about reached the point where blind, impulsive action would take over; where they would be impossible to reason with any longer. Without looking back at the crowd, Dillon let himself into the jail office and locked the door behind him.

Out on the street, once again the Galloway mob began their crazy chanting: "We want Gant! We want Gant!"

Sitting on a chair, facing the door, Chester sat with a shotgun across his knees. His thin face was pale and tightly drawn with strain.

"Gosh, Mr. Dillon, am I glad to see you! I didn't know what to do. That loony bunch out there wanted me to come out and talk things over with them. But I stayed right here. I was afraid they might grab me."

"You did right, Chester. For a moment I was afraid they were going to try to grab me. Galloway's got them so

bloodthirsty for a hanging they don't have much sense left."

"What are we going to do, Mr. Dillon? They'll finally reach the point where nothing'll stop 'em, won't they?"

"I'm afraid so. But at least we've got an hour. They've given us another hour."

Briefly the Marshal was torn by despair. One hour. What good was one hour going to do him? What was he going to do with it?

"If they ever do storm this place, I'm afraid we won't be able to stop 'em, Mr. Dillon."

"I know it, Chester." Then Dillon remembered about the horse Nick Root had found. He walked over to the cell where Jan Gant had been standing, looking out through the bars, listening to them talk. Gant's face was now haggard with dread.

For a moment he stood there looking at Gant, and then Dillon said abruptly, "Well, Gant, we've found your friend, Vince Huggins."

"You did?" Gant's face lighted with hope. "What—what did he say, Marshal? Did he say anything that would help me?"

"I don't know." Carefully Dillon studied Gant's face. "He's dead."

"Oh, no!" Gant gasped. "Did you have to shoot him, Marshal?"

"What makes you think he was shot?"

"Well, how else would he die? What difference does that make, anyhow. The main thing is, did you find the money on him, Marshal?"

Right then and there Dillon knew that Jan Gant was innocent. He was positive of it. He was sure the man wasn't acting. And if Gant had been in on the robbery with Huggins, then killed him afterward, so as to keep all the loot, he would have known Huggins didn't have the money on his body.

"No, Jan," Dillon said. "In fact, I was just sort of testing you, to see if you've been lying to us. I'm convinced now that you haven't. I really and completely believe in you now, Jan Gant."

Gant looked puzzled. "Then you didn't find Huggins? He—he isn't dead?"

"You can probably tell me that, Jan. Do you remember anything about the horse Huggins was riding? Can you describe him?"

Gant thought about it a moment. Then he said, "Yes. It was a black gelding with an odd-shaped blaze on his forehead. It was shaped like a—like a four-leaf clover. That's it."

"Uh-huh. How about the saddle and trappings. Anything about those?"

"Well, only that they had some brass trimmings."

"That does it," Dillon said. "It was Huggins' horse that Nick Root had."

He told Gant and Chester about the incident with Root. When he had finished, Chester said, "That makes it look to me as though Huggins and somebody else worked together to rob and kill the old man. Then when they finished, the other party shot Huggins as they mounted to ride away."

"That's the way I see it, too, Chester. But Huggins didn't die immediately. He stayed in the saddle long enough to drip blood on it, before he fell off."

"Maybe he didn't die, Marshal. Was only wounded."

"I doubt it. He couldn't have gone far, wounded that way, without a horse. Somebody would have picked him up. We'd have heard about it. . . . The way it looks to me is that whoever shot Huggins buried him, probably somewhere around the Foster place. Tomorrow we'll go out there and look around. I'm almost sure we'll find Huggins' grave. . . . But that's tomorrow. We've got to find out to-night who the man with Huggins was, Chester. Within one hour, if we can!"

"Leapin' catfish, Mr. Dillon, how we goin' to do it?"

"I wish I knew, Chester. I sure wish I knew."

13   *An Important Clue*

The next moment Marshal Dillon noticed that Chester was flipping a coin, a nervous habit he sometimes exhibited. Dillon saw that the coin was a silver dollar. He said, "Chester, where'd you get that cartwheel? Is that one of those we found in Jeff Foster's money box?"

"Why, no, Mr. Dillon." Chester looked hurt. "You know I wouldn't do anything like that—touch any official evidence. Especially money. I don't take money that doesn't belong to me, Mr. Dillon, you ought to know that."

"I'm sorry, Chester. I didn't mean to hurt your feelings. But where did you get it? Do you remember?"

"Why, sure. I just got it today. Got it at the Long Branch, when I stopped in to have a root beer and talk with Miss Kitty a spell. Why, Mr. Dillon?"

"I'm not sure, Chester. But you know we haven't seen

many cartwheels like that here in Dodge lately. Not since they minted that last batch several years ago. Why, come to think of it, I haven't seen one in weeks."

Chester scratched his head, frowning. "No, neither have I. I hadn't thought about that. I wonder where it came from."

"I've got to find out. It may not do much good but at least it's something to look into, Chester. We can't overlook anything at this late stage. . . . I'm going to leave by the rear door so that bunch outside won't know I'm not still here."

Chester looked worriedly toward the street door as once again the waiting Galloway mob yelled something. "You goin' to be very long, Mr. Dillon?"

"I don't think so, Chester. I'll get back inside an hour, anyhow."

Leaving the jail building by the rear exit, Dillon moved through alleys until he came to the rear entrance of the Long Branch. At the back door, he asked one of the kitchen workers to bring the bartender back there to talk with him.

"Don't let anyone at the bar know I'm out here," Dillon warned the man.

"No, sir, I won't, Mr. Dillon."

The kitchen worker left, and in a few moments the neat-looking bartender with the handle-bar mustaches came to the back door. "You wanted to see me, Marshal?"

"Yes, Charlie. I want you to think carefully now. It's important. Did you get paid by any customer today with a silver dollar?"

Charlie pulled at his lower lip, thinking. Finally he looked up. "Yeah, Marshal, so happens I did. I remember one being in the cash register."

"Do you remember who gave it to you?"

The bartender thought again. Then he shook his head. "I'm tryin' to think. I'm afraid not, Marshal. We've been so blamed busy I—"

"I know," Dillon said. "I sure wish you could remember, though. Later on you gave that same silver dollar in change to Chester. Do you remember that?"

"Yes. Yes, now I do. Wait a minute. It couldn't have been too long before that I took it in. Hold it a minute, Marshal. I think I'm beginning to—yes, now I remember. At the time I wondered where he'd gotten it from. What's his name again—that big, ugly, kind o' slow-witted feller sometimes hangs out with the Galloway crowd? In fact he was with 'em today. Oh, yeah. Jumbo. Jumbo Jones."

"I see. You're certain, Charlie? This is very important."

"I'm sure, Marshal. Now I am. It comes back quite clear to me."

"Thanks, Charlie. You've been a big help."

"Glad to oblige, Marshal."

"But, Charlie, don't tell anybody about this—nor that I've been here tonight. You understand?"

"If you say so, Marshal. I'll keep mum about it."

Dillon waved good-by and left. He went through an alley and came out onto the street behind Front Street. At the next block he turned down a side street. In three or four blocks he was out of the rooming-house district and at the western edge of the town. Here there were only a few scattered old shacks and some odd tents pitched, at the edge of the prairie. Dillon walked up to the nearest shack, outside of which sat a bearded, very old man, dressed in dirty, half-rotted buckskins.

"Good evenin', sir," Dillon said. "I'm looking for a man called Jumbo Jones. Can you tell me which of these shacks is his?"

The old man stared up at Dillon, while he puffed thoughtfully on an old corncob pipe. Finally he said, "You be Marshal Dillon, ain't you?"

Dillon nodded. "That's right."

The old man squinted his eyes. "Ain't never seen you before. Heard about you. Heard lot of good things about you, Marshal. You're a pretty big man, ain't you? Don't see many fellers as big as you. Now I remember there was a man I once knew, a third cousin, I think it was, on my wife's side, anyhow, he—"

"I'm sorry to have to interrupt you, old-timer," Dillon said, smiling. "We can have a long talk some other time. Right now I'm in kind of a hurry."

"Oh? On official business out here, are ye?"

"Yes, sir. You were goin' to tell me where Jumbo Jones lives."

"What's he done, Marshal? Jumbo ain't got much sense, and if he hangs around that Galloway bunch too much, he'll sure get into trouble. But he ain't a really bad boy, neither."

"I know. Now, where does he live?"

The old man gestured with one arm. "Down there. Last shack down that way. Probably ain't there, though. Probably in town somewheres. Might be workin', even. He's a swamper in one o' them saloon places, y'know."

"I know. Thanks, old-timer." Dillon started away.

"Don't mention it. Pleasure. Ain't often I get a chance to help the law on official business." The old man chuckled softly. "Stop by again sometime, Marshal, when you can set a spell. I don't get much company. Gets mighty lonesome sometimes."

Dillon waved and called back, "I'll try to do that."

The hut where Jumbo Jones lived had been put together with odd pieces of lumber taken from various sources. There were even some barrel staves nailed together to form part of one wall. Dried mud had been used to fill in chinks between boards. There was no light on in the place as Dillon walked up to the open door. He stood just outside and called, "Jumbo! You in there?"

For a moment there was no answer, but then, just as Dillon was about to shout again, a voice inside said sleepily, "Who is it? Who's out there?"

"It's Marshal Dillon, Jumbo. Put on a light. I want to come in and talk to you."

Bedsprings creaked inside and there was the sound of somebody moving about. At the same time Jumbo said, "Reckon I was sleepin', Marshal. I do a lot of sleepin' when I'm not workin', y'know. I work so hard on the job I'm plumb tired out when I'm off. . . . Just a moment and

I'll have this persnickety old lamp fired up."

A glow of light showed inside and grew brighter as a lampwick caught full fire. Dillon stepped inside the hut. Jumbo Jones, a man in his late twenties and built like a gorilla, with long powerful arms and short, stocky, bowed legs, was just pulling on a pair of trousers. His moonlike face was covered at the cheeks and chin with a three-day growth of blond stubble. His yellow hair was a thick tangle on his flat-crowned head. His thick lips were pulled back in a grin, exposing large, strong, but dingy-looking teeth.

"You ain't never visited me before, Marshal. How do you like my place? Of course, it ain't anything fancy, but it's mine."

Dillon looked briefly around. The hut was furnished with odds and ends of junk but looked surprisingly clean and well-kept.

"It looks just fine, Jumbo," Dillon said. "I've got some questions to ask you, if you're awake enough. I'll want some straight answers, Jumbo, so you'll have to think hard."

"Why, sure, Marshal," Jumbo said. He gestured toward a packing crate. "Have a seat. What you want to ask me, Marshal?"

"Did Mike Galloway spend the night here, last night?"

Jumbo rubbed the heel of his hand hard into the long hair over his ears. He cast his eyes up toward the ceiling. "Last night?" He pondered the matter. "Let me see. Oh, yeah, last night. Sure he did, Marshal. We was at a poker game together, me and ol' Mike. I didn't play, of course, Marshal. Nobody'll let me play cards with them. Maybe because I never have any money, huh, Marshal? Anyhow, after we finished playing cards, we came home here. Mike Galloway, he said he was afeared to sleep at his own place. Said he was afraid Jan Gant might come after him. He was afraid of that Jan Gant, Marshal."

"I know, Jumbo. And Galloway stayed here at your place all night? You sure he didn't leave later? He was still here in the morning when you woke up?"

"Mmmm-hmmm. I'm positive about that, Marshal."

"You know I don't like it when you lie to me, Jumbo. You sure you're telling the truth this time?"

Jumbo Jones crossed his powerfully muscled arms over his chest. "Cross my heart, Marshal." He laughed. It was a soft, easy sound, like a child's innocent laughter. "I don't ever try to lie to you any more, Marshal. You always catch me when I do. You know that, Marshal. I haven't tried to lie to you in a long time. What's the sense to it when you catch me at it every single time?"

From past experience, Matt Dillon could tell that Jumbo was telling the truth. When he was lying, the big man always fidgeted and twisted his large feet this way and that. He tried to control this but he never could. He was standing still and steady now, as he answered Dillon's questions.

"There's one other thing," Dillon said, then. "You had a silver dollar today, Jumbo. You spent it at the Long Branch. Where'd you get that money, Jumbo?"

Jumbo's gaze turned away from Dillon. He shifted his feet. His hands began to twitch at his sides. Finally he said, "I don't know what you're talkin' about, Marshal. I haven't had any silver money. You must mean somebody else, Marshal."

"I mean you, Jumbo. And this time you aren't telling the truth. I want the truth, Jumbo. Where'd you get that silver dollar?"

Still Jumbo's eyes kept shifting away from Dillon's steady gaze. "Oh, yes, now I do remember, Marshal. I—I'd forgotten about that ol' silver dollar. Sure, now. Well, I— you see, I found it, Marshal."

Dillon looked down at Jumbo's shuffling feet. "Try

again, Jumbo. You didn't find that coin. Where did you get it?"

Suddenly Jumbo blurted out, "Well, I did find it, in a way—sort of, Marshal. Did—did Mike Galloway send you out here to arrest me for stealin' that cartwheel, Marshal? If he did, I'll never be friends with Mike Galloway again. Because I didn't really steal it."

"But the silver dollar did belong to Galloway?"

"I suppose so. I mean, I don't know for sure but it *must* have been his. Nobody else has been out here. I found it under the bunk where Mike slept last night. I should have told him about it, I suppose, and give it back to him. I guess not doin' that makes it like I stole it from him—even though he didn't seem to know he'd lost it. I—I'll give it back to him though, out of my next pay. I promise, Marshal. You aren't going to arrest me for stealing that silver dollar, are you?"

"No, Jumbo. Not this time. But in the future you must always return anything valuable that you find."

"Gosh, thanks, Marshal," Jumbo said. He finger-combed his thick, yellow hair. "You got any more questions, Marshal? 'Cause if you haven't, I got to go into town. There's goin' to be a hangin', Marshal. They're goin' to hang Gant."

"No, they aren't, Jumbo. If that's all you're going in for, you can save yourself the trip."

Dillon was silent then for a few moments. He couldn't figure this out. Galloway's having a silver dollar at a time like this could be just a coincidence. Or it could mean that Mike Galloway was Huggins' partner in the slaying of Jeff Foster. Yet that would be impossible if Jumbo was telling the truth about Galloway spending the night here. And Dillon was sure that Jumbo wasn't lying about that.

Then all of a sudden the explanation came to Dillon. It was one of those simple explanations that could be overlooked because of its utter simplicity.

Dillon said, "Jumbo, do you sleep very heavy?"

"Huh?" Jumbo scratched his head. "Heavy? How do you mean, Marshal?"

"I mean do you wake easily? Do noises disturb you when you're sleeping soundly?"

Jumbo laughed. "Oh, no, Marshal. Somebody once told me I sleep like the dead. They said if I was fast asleep, you could blow this place up with gunpowder and I'd sleep right through it. I remember once—"

"Wait a minute, Jumbo," Dillon cut in. "Then if Mike Galloway got up last night and went someplace and came back before morning and was in bed again before you waked up, you wouldn't even know he'd gone out. Would you?"

Jumbo frowned. He said, "Well, maybe not, Marshal. No, I guess something like that wouldn't wake me. But why would Mike Galloway want to do something like that? Where would he go in the middle of the night?"

"That's a good question, Jumbo. And I think I know the answer."

Just then a kitten, tiger-striped and fluffy, came skittering playfully through the doorway into the hut. It went leaping and cavorting about the room and then pounced on something near one wall and picked it up between its paws.

"That's Candy, my cat," Jumbo said proudly. "I named her that because she's got stripes like a stick o' candy. Ain't she pretty, Marshal?"

"Cute little kitty, all right," Dillon agreed. He squatted down and drummed his fingers on the floor, trying to get the kitten's attention. But it was too busy, playing with the thing it had picked up off the floor.

"What's that thing she's playing with?" Dillon asked. "Looks like a bird feather? She kill a bird?"

"No," Jumbo said. "I don't know where it come from, Marshal. We don't have any green birds around here. We don't have any birds with feathers that big. Candy, she found that green feather under that bunk over there this morning."

Just then the kitten lost interest in playing with the feather and dropped it from her mouth. She scampered out the door again. Dillon walked over and picked up the feather. He smoothed it out between his fingers.

"A green feather," he mused. "Hmmmmm! What kind of birds have green feathers, Jumbo?"

Jumbo shrugged. "I don't know. I've never seen any green birds. A canary, maybe, Marshal?"

"Not with a feather this size. I'll tell you what kind of bird I think it came from. It could have come from a parrot, Jumbo."

The other man's thick blond eyebrows knit together. "You must be wrong, Marshal. We don't have any parrots around here."

"I know. Who slept in the bunk where the kitten found this feather?"

"Mike Galloway, Marshal. I meant to ask him where it came from, but I forgot."

"I'm glad you did, Jumbo. Very glad. . . . Well, I've got to get back to the jailhouse. Thanks for answering my questions."

"That's all right, Marshal. So long." Jumbo waved as he watched the Marshal walk out the door of the shack.

As Dillon stepped out into the darkness, something whistled near his right ear. Then there was a ringing pain in that side of his head. The sky—full of stars now— seemed to tilt and spin and then all the stars went out. There was just blackness. . . .

14   *Fire!*

Shortly after Marshal Dillon left him, the old man in buckskins saw another figure moving through the dark toward the shack of Jumbo Jones. At that distance, in the dark, the old man couldn't see who it was.

He pulled gently at his gray beard and stared in that direction. To himself he said, "That Jumbo's certainly havin' a lot of company tonight. First that Marshal feller, Matt Dillon—nice feller, too—and now this other person, whoever it is. I wish I could have a lot of company like that. Nobody much ever comes to see me. Even the Marshal wouldn't have stopped by if he hadn't had to ask for directions."

The old man looked up at the stars. "Well, I've always got the stars for company, when I sit out here nights. Sometimes the man in the moon too. Funny thing but I don't seem to feel lonely, except after somebody's visited me."

Then he stopped talking to himself and just sat, staring into the darkness and occasionally lighting and puffing on his corncob pipe. Several times he caught himself dozing, almost falling off the box he was sitting on. Then he murmured, "Here, here now, Jasper! None of that. You want to sleep, go on in and get into bed like any sensible person would do."

After one of these awakenings, he looked toward Jumbo Jones's shack and wondered if perhaps it was Jumbo's birthday or something, since he was having all that company come to see him, two people at the same time. Then he saw one of the visitors leave Jumbo's shack and head toward town. He still couldn't see who it was.

"Well, that feller didn't stay long, that's for sure."

A few moments later, old Jasper raised his head and sniffed the air suspiciously. He thought he smelled smoke. He looked around to see if any of the other shack dwellers were burning garbage. He didn't see any sign of a fire.

"By golly," Jasper told himself, "that's strange, all right. I've heard of folks seein' things but this is the first time I ever heard of a body *smellin'* things." He chuckled.

Then he sniffed the air again. "By gum, it is too smoke.

I know it this time. I ain't just imaginin' it. . . . Still can't figure where it's comin' from, though."

Jasper kept looking around. Finally, shielding his eyes with one hand, he stared toward Jumbo Jones's place.

"Now what in thunderation kind of lamp is that, Jumbo's burnin' up there?" he asked himself. "Never seen him use such a bright light. . . . It keeps gettin' brighter all the time too."

Then the wind blew the smell of smoke so strongly it almost choked Jasper, made him cough as he breathed it in. The next instant he saw where the smoke was coming from.

The "lamp" inside the Jones cabin was now so bright, it sent a great splash of light out the open front door. It illuminated the clouds of black smoke that had begun to roll through the opening.

"Well, if that don't beat all!" Jasper cried. "Jumbo's place is on fire!"

The old man stood up, waving his arms in wild excitement. He hobbled around in a circle, shouting, "Hey, somebody! Fire! Fire!"

Nobody answered him; nobody heard. Jasper remembered then that most of the men who lived in the other shacks didn't come back from town until later. If anything was going to be done about that fire, he would have to do it himself. He began to hobble toward the burning shack.

He wondered why Jumbo Jones and his other visitor didn't come out. He figured that they were probably still trying to put out the fire. Well, Jasper thought that he would give them a hand. He began to move a little faster.

Close to Jumbo's shack now, he had to throw his arm up across his face to keep from breathing in the thick smoke. He could hear the crackle of flames inside the shack. He shouted, "Hey, you in there! Jumbo! Need any help? Ol' Jasper's comin' to give you a hand. Used to be a fire fighter in my younger days."

There was no answer from inside the burning shack. Reaching the doorway, Jasper staggered back for a moment, halted by the blasting heat. Then he moved forward again, until he could see inside the place. He shouted in surprise, then, for there were two figures sprawled out on the floor inside the shack. He saw, too, that the rear of the shack was now a solid wall of flames that was beginning to creep across the room, following a trail of spilled oil from the lamp that lay shattered on the floor.

"Both of 'em overcome by the smoke, by gum!" Jasper

said. "I got to get 'em out o' there before they get burned up like slabs of toast!"

Moving as fast as his stiffened muscles would permit, he tugged off his thick woolen shirt. He wrapped it around his head below the eyes, and then he hobbled through the doorway.

Marshal Dillon, with a lump swelling over his right temple, was nearest the door. Jasper tackled him first. No matter how hard he tugged, he couldn't seem to budge the big, husky figure of the Marshal more than a few inches at a time. And every few moments he had to move back and drag Jumbo Jones farther away from the flames creeping across the floor.

But finally he got the Marshal's limp, unconscious figure to the doorsill and tumbled him outside. Not losing any time, he went back in after Jumbo Jones. But Jasper was almost exhausted now. The smoke was beginning to penetrate through the mask he had made with the shirt. Several times he felt as though he was going to suffocate. Jumbo Jones's dead weight seemed to get heavier and heavier. Jasper was able to move it only about an inch at a time. Three walls of the house were now in flames and more than half the floor was burning. Most of the articles of furniture had already begun to burn.

Then somebody said, between coughing spells, "I'll help you, old-timer."

Jasper looked up to see the smoke-blackened face of Marshal Dillon. "Glory be!" he cried in a muffled voice. "The fresh air brought you to in time to help me."

With the Marshal's help, Jumbo, too, was soon dragged out into the fresh air. Jasper unwrapped his shirt from around his head and put it back on. While he did this, Dillon said, "I wish I knew how to thank you, old-timer. That was a mighty brave thing to do at your age."

"Here now, Marshal," Jasper said, pulling in his chin and puffing out his chest. "I ain't so old, really. Since when's eighty-six years make a man old."

"I'm sorry, Jasper. It was a brave thing for a man of any age to do."

Both of them looked around then, as one side of the burning shack caved in with a roar.

"Didn't make it a minute too soon, by gum!" Jasper said. Then he looked down at Jumbo Jones. "He's still out cold, Marshal. And look at his shoes and the bottom of his jeans, all scorched. Appears like maybe his feet and legs got burned a little."

"Yeah," Dillon said. "Can I take him into your place, Jasper? When I get back to town I'll send Doc Adams out to have a look at him."

"Sure thing, Marshal."

Holding Jumbo under the arms, Dillon dragged him over to Jasper's shack and lugged him inside. He lifted him up onto an old iron-poster bed. Then he felt Jumbo's pulse.

"What happened over to his place anyhow, Marshal? How'd that fire get started and spread so fast, with the two of you right there?"

"I can't tell you very much," Dillon said as he removed Jumbo's shoes. "Jumbo's feet are blistered a little but not as bad as they might be. Doc will be able to fix them up, all right."

"What you mean, you don't know, Marshal? You was there!"

"All I can tell you is this, Jasper. I was just leaving. I started out the door, and the moment I got outside something banged me on the side of the head and knocked me out." He reached up and tenderly touched the lump at his temple.

"You mean somebody was waitin' out there for you?"

"That's about it, old-timer. The rest of it, about the fire,

I don't know any more about that than you do. We'll have
to hear that from Jumbo, if he ever comes around." Dillon
felt the back of Jumbo's head. "He's got a lump back here."

"Then somebody must've conked him on the head too.
Now, who'd want to do a thing like that, Marshal—knock
both of you out and leave you there to burn? What kind
of critter could be that low-down?"

Before Dillon could answer, Jasper said, "Marshal, he's
beginnin' to blink his eyes. Jumbo's among the livin' again."

A moment later, still looking dazed, Jumbo Jones sat up.
He put his hand to the back of his head and then looked
down at his feet.

"My feet!" he cried. "My feet are all burned!"

"Now take it easy, Jumbo," Dillon told him. "You'll be
all right. Later I'll have Doc Adams come out and take care
of those feet for you, but right now I've got to ask you a
couple of questions, Jumbo."

Jumbo looked around dazedly. "What am I doing here?
Why aren't we at my place, Marshal?"

"Your shack is burned down, Jumbo."

"Burned—" Jumbo stared at Dillon, openmouthed. Then
his eyes began to clear. "Now I'm beginning to remember.
Where—where's Mike Galloway? Why did he knock us

out, Marshal? Why, I—I was never so surprised in my life
as I was when right after you stepped out the door, Mike
comes draggin' you back in, knocked cold. Then, before
I could find out what was goin' on, he slams me with the
butt of his gun. What would he do a thing like that for,
Marshal?"

"So he could leave us there to burn to death after he
smashed the kerosene lamp on the floor and started the
fire, Jumbo."

"Is that what he did, Marshal?"

Jasper clucked his tongue. "Never heard of anything
like that in my life. I knew that Mike Galloway was a
bad one, all I've heard about him. But why would he do a
thing like that?"

"To save his own hide," Dillon said. "Listen, I've got
to go back to the jailhouse. Will you be all right until Doc
Adams gets here, Jumbo? How are your feet?"

Jumbo winced. "Gettin' mighty painful but I guess I
can stand it. You goin' to get Mike Galloway for doin'
that to us, Marshal?"

"I hope so, Jumbo." Dillon turned to Jasper and stuck
out his hand. "I want to thank you again. You did a fine,
brave thing. I'm going to see that everyone in Dodge hears

about it, Jasper. If you ever need a favor of any kind, I'm the man to ask. You'll get it."

"Why, that's mighty pleasant of you, Marshal." Jasper looked toward the bed where Jumbo was sitting. "At least I've got some company for a little while. It's an ill wind that doesn't blow some good for somebody, eh, Marshal? Heh-heh!"

"Guess that's one way of looking at it. Be seeing you."

Dillon left Jasper's shack and started back toward town. As he walked, the night wind cool on his blackened face, the Marshal thought back on all that had happened. He knew for sure now that Mike Galloway had been the man with Huggins, and that the two of them had been responsible for the murder and robbery of Uncle Jeff Foster.

He knew it, the Marshal reflected, but he still had no conclusive proof. The one small bit of evidence he had had —the parrot feather which must have got caught in Galloway's clothing the night before—was now burned in Jumbo's shack.

The silver dollar wasn't conclusive proof of anything, really. The only thing the Marshal really had on Galloway was this murderous attack tonight. And they only had Jumbo's word on that. If Galloway denied it, a court would be more likely to take his word than Jumbo's.

But at least he knew now, for sure, Dillon told himself. There could be no other reason for Galloway's actions. As he reached the edge of town and hurried on down a side street, the Marshal prayed that somehow he would get the evidence he needed.

15   *Crisis at the Jailhouse*

When he left the burning shack of Jumbo Jones, Mike Galloway congratulated himself on how fine everything seemed to be working out in his favor. It was a good thing, he told himself, that someone in the lynch mob had wondered if there was a rear door to the jailhouse building, and if so, whether Dillon might not use it to spirit Jan Gant away, if the mob tried to break into the front of the building.

It had been another stroke of luck that Galloway had gone around the back of the building to investigate that possibility, just as the Marshal was coming out. At first Galloway had trailed the Marshal, thinking that he might be going to deputize some men to help him protect the jail.

Galloway had been pretty nervous as he listened to Dillon's conversation with the bartender of the Long Branch at the back of the kitchen, and learned about that fool Jumbo finding one of old Foster's silver dollars.

He had been even more scared after listening outside Jumbo's shack and realizing that Dillon finally knew for sure that he was the killer. He knew then that he had to do something drastic to protect himself. Knocking them both out and setting fire to the place was a master stroke of genius, he told himself. Now he had nothing at all to worry about. Nobody could connect him with the fire. It would just be one of those tragic accidents.

All that remained to be done was to settle with Jan Gant, by seeing the man strung up proper to a tree, and everything would be nicely rounded out.

Of course, if he wanted to have a good time spending some of old Jeff Foster's money, it would be best to go up to Abilene, to make sure he didn't rouse any suspicions about his sudden wealth.

As Galloway came out onto Front Street once more and turned toward the jail building, he saw that his crowd of followers had thinned out considerably.

He went up to the fifteen or twenty men who were left, anger rising in him. "What happened to the others?" he demanded, looking around him.

"They drifted off, one by one," a burly, black-bearded mule skinner said. "They thought you'd run out on us. Where in tarnation you been so long, Mike? We thought you just went around to see about that back door."

"I did. But then I caught the Marshal sneakin' out of it and I followed him," Galloway explained. "I was afraid he might be goin' to try to deputize some help and I wanted to see what he was up to."

"What was he? Where did he go?"

"I trailed him to the rear of the Long Branch but when he left there, I lost him. I don't know where he went after that. I checked at a few places but couldn't catch up with him again. Then I came back here."

"What are we going to do now, Mike? We need a bigger crowd. As a matter of fact, a lot of the ones who're left have sort of lost their taste for this hangin'."

Galloway glared around at the others. "Oh, is that so?" he roared. "And I thought I had some real men on my side in this thing! I leave you for a little while and you're all ready to turn tail like a pack of yellow curs and run out on me. And you call yourselves men! More like a bunch of old women, you're actin' like, if you ask me."

The men looked sheepish. Nobody said anything.

"All right!" Galloway told them. "Go ahead! Run out on me, but listen to this—if none of you still want to see justice done, *I do!* I'm going to see poor old Jeff Foster's death avenged, if I have to do it all by myself. If I have to break into that jailhouse all by my lonesome and drag that murderin', thievin' Jan Gant out and personally put a rope around his neck, I'll do it!"

"You're talkin' big now, Mike," one of the crowd told him, "but when Marshal Dillon stands up to us, I've noticed you back down and start stalling for time."

"That's a lie!" Galloway thundered, cords standing out in his thick neck. He shook a big fist at the man who spoke. "The Marshal! That's all I hear in this town—the Marshal, the Marshal! You'd think Dillon was some kind of supernatural being or something. It isn't Dillon, the man, I've been standing back for—it's Dillon, The Law. I'm a law-respectin' man—we all are. So we had to give the law its full chance. Well, the law's had its chance now. The hour I gave Dillon is more than up. So now we're through waiting."

Galloway looked around at the faces watching him. He saw that his words were getting through to them. It wasn't going to take much more to work them up to a frenzy again. Galloway—like all rabble-rousers, men who arouse a mob to violence for their own selfish purposes—knew the kind of people he was dealing with. He knew that most of those who join a mob do so because of a weakness within themselves that makes them look for a false strength in mob-power. He knew what they wanted to hear.

"I'm not afraid of Marshal Dillon," Galloway shouted. "I'll prove that. Right now I'm going to walk up to that jailhouse door and demand that Gant be turned over to us for trial. There'll be no more stalling. If they refuse, we'll break in and drag that murderin' coyote out of there. And I'll be the first one in the bunch. If anyone gets hurt, it'll be me. I'm willing to sacrifice my own life to see that justice is handed out the way it should be in Dodge City!"

The men looked at each other with nods of agreement. Several of them cheered.

Hitching up his belt, his jaw set firmly, Galloway swaggered toward the door of the jailhouse building. "That's the end of the talkin'," he called back to the mob. "From now on there'll be nothing but action!"

He stood with feet firmly planted in front of the jailhouse door and pounded on it with both fists.

"Listen to me, in there! This is Mike Galloway. Your

time is up. We want Gant and we want him now! We'll give you until the count of ten to throw him out here to us. If you don't, we're coming in to get him. Nothing's going to stop us—not words, not guns!"

On the street behind him, the crowd cheered wildly.

Mike Galloway counted slowly to ten. There was no answer from within the jailhouse. Galloway turned away from the door.

"All right, men! They've had their chance to co-operate." He walked toward the hitching rail in front of the jail. "We'll need a battering ram to break down the door. How about this hitching rail? Some of you help me tear it loose."

A dozen men joined Galloway in wrapping their arms around the stout length of timber that formed the hitching rail. They yanked and jerked in unison and soon the rail was torn loose from the uprights. Then the same men held the length of timber as a battering ram and moved up to the jailhouse door.

Galloway, up at the front, shouted, "All right! Here we go! Heave ho!"

The battering ram crashed hard against the door. The door shuddered and splintered but held firm. The men moved back and ran forward again. And this time the

door smashed in and open, to hang from one hinge. Gallo-way and the others dropped the battering ram and crowded into the doorway.

Inside they saw Chester Good standing in front of one of the cells, holding a single-barreled shotgun pointed straight at the door. Chester's long, thin jaw was ridged tight with muscle. His face was pale as parchment. Behind him, Jan Gant pressed against the bars of his cell.

"All right," Chester said, his voice trembling but determined. "That's as far as you come. The first man who takes another step into this building gets shot."

Mike Galloway smiled disarmingly. He said, "Oh, come on now, Chester. You wouldn't shoot any of your fellow citizens, would you? Put that gun down, Chester. We've got nothing against you. Just stand back out of the way and you won't get hurt."

"I've got my job to do," Chester answered. "I intend to do it, no matter what! You just stand back, Galloway!"

"Why, sure you want to do your job, Chester. And you've done it, haven't you? You *tried* to keep us out. But nobody expects a man to get killed, doing his job, do they, Chester?"

Chester's long, thin face was glistening with perspiration. But the big shotgun in his hands never wavered. It stayed pointed right at Galloway's chest.

"I won't be the first to die," Chester answered. "I'm aimin' to do just what Mr. Dillon would do. If you make another move, I'll shoot you first, Galloway. And I'm afraid that a shotgun blast won't hit you, alone. If some of you others want to die with Galloway, why you—you're crazier than I think you are. Some of you other men have families. What in blazes has got into you-all, doin' a thing like this? Why don't you forget about it, and go on home to your families where you belong?"

There was a stirring of unrest in the mob jammed against the doorway behind Galloway, peering over his shoulders.

"That's a fine speech, Chester," Galloway said quickly. "Almost as good a one as Dillon would make. Where is the good Marshal, by the way, Chester?"

"I—well—I don't know for sure. He'll probably be back any minute."

"Will he, Chester? Maybe you're wrong about that. Maybe Marshal Dillon figured it out that he wasn't going to be able to stop us and just ran out, leavin' you holdin' the bag, Chester."

Chester shook his head hard. "Mr. Dillon wouldn't do anything like that!"

"Wouldn't he, Chester? Looks to me as though he has! Now step aside and throw me your keys, or do you want me to come over there and take them away from you? We can't waste any more time on small talk."

Galloway took a tentative step forward.

Chester backed up against the steel bars behind him and shifted the weight of the shotgun in his hands. But he still kept it pointed right at Galloway. Behind Galloway, their nerve bolstered by their leader's confident manner and forward move, some of the other men edged inside the doorway.

Chester pleaded then, sweat running down his lean cheeks, "Please, Mr. Galloway, don't make me shoot you! I don't want to kill anybody if I can help it. You know that. But I've got to, if you keep pressin' me. I can only be pressed so far, Galloway. . . . Some of you others—grab him, stop him before he gets himself killed! I'm warning you!"

"Yes, sir, Chester," Galloway went on, just as though Chester hadn't spoken, "Marshal Dillon is a lot smarter man than I gave him credit for. He had more sense than to stay here and try to stop us. He got out while the gettin' was good—even if he did stick you with the part of his job he didn't have the guts to do himself. He must've figured you had more courage than he did. It looks like he was right, Chester—even though that courage seems a little foolhardy, right now. Doesn't it?"

"That's not so!" Chester cried. "Something's holding Mr. Dillon up. He wouldn't run out on me. He's never run out on trouble in his whole life. He'll be back here any minute. You wait and see."

"We're through waitin' on Dillon!" Galloway made a beckoning move with his arm. "Let's go, men. Follow me. I'm walkin' up to Chester and takin' that gun away from him."

From behind Chester, Jan Gant said, "Chester, you're going to get yourself killed for nothing. Even if you shoot some of them, the rest will come on and get me. Maybe you'd better let them take me, Chester."

"Now, there's a man with sense, even if he is a low-down, thievin' killer of weak and harmless old men!" Galloway said.

"No, sir!" Chester said determinedly. "I—I'm not lettin' Mr. Dillon down!"

"Even though he's let you down, Chester?"

Before Chester could answer, there was the sound of a door opening in the rear of the building. Footsteps sounded and then the tall, big-shouldered figure of Marshal Dillon, his strong-looking face even more awesomely determined than usual, dirty and smoke-blackened as it was, walked up beside Chester. Dillon held his forty-four in his hand.

"You know I wouldn't do a thing like that, Galloway," Dillon said softly.

16   *Dead End*

For one long, staggering moment, Mike Galloway looked as though he was going to drop in a dead faint. His eyes almost bugged from his head. His throat muscles worked violently as he tried to swallow. His lips opened and moved and he tried to talk but could not get out any words. He raised a trembling hand and passed it across his eyes as though to clear his vision.

"What's the trouble, Mike?" Dillon asked. "Cat got your tongue all of a sudden? What's happened to all your big talk?"

Still Mike Galloway stood speechless, staring.

"Gosh, but I sure am mighty glad to see you, Mr. Dillon," Chester said.

"You seem to be about the only one who is, Chester. Doesn't strike me that Galloway's very happy about it, at all. . . . Mike, that fire didn't do the job you wanted it to do. Maybe Jumbo and I are too tough to burn."

"I—I don't know what you're talkin' about," Galloway finally managed to say.

"What in the world's the matter with him, Mr. Dillon?" Chester asked. "He looks at you as though he's seein' a ghost."

"He probably thinks he is, Chester. He did his best to kill me—and Jumbo Jones. Yes, Galloway, *he's* alive too. I don't reckon he thinks you're such a hero any more."

Galloway looked around at some of the men with him. They were all staring at him curiously. He began to recover somewhat from the shock of seeing Dillon and tried to bluff his way through the situation.

"Dillon's crazy, I tell you. He's talkin' riddles. What's he tryin' to put over here, anyhow? Listen to me, men! It's just another trick to stall us off."

"Sure, Galloway." Dillon pointed to his face. "I guess I smoked up my own face—and gave myself this lump on the temple?" Quickly he told what had happened out at Jumbo Jones's shack.

When he had finished, Galloway yelled, "What kind of wild, loco story is that, Dillon? Do you expect these men to believe that? I tell you, this is all a trick! You say I tried to kill you and Jumbo because you'd learned that me and Huggins were the ones who killed Jeff Foster. And I say, back up your words, Marshal. Show some proof!"

Dillon told about the silver dollar, about finding the green parrot feather.

"You'll have to do better than that, Marshal," Galloway told him. "What kind of flimsy evidence is that? You're just making a last-minute, desperate effort to save the life of your friend Gant, by pinning his crime on me and Huggins. Well, Huggins is a dead man and can't defend himself, but I sure can. I—"

"Wait a minute, Galloway," Dillon butted in. "You just said Huggins is dead. How do you know that? I didn't say anything about Huggins being dead."

"Well, I—I don't know. I j-just figured he was, I suppose," Galloway blustered. "What difference does that make? I still say you haven't any proof against me."

"You're mistaken, Galloway. I've got proof, all right. Plenty of it. A couple of thousand dollars' worth of it."

Galloway looked shaken. Quickly, he crossed one arm in front of his stomach as though to protect himself against a blow there. He said, his voice beginning to break with fear, "I—I'm gettin' out of here. This man's crazy. Next thing you know, he'll shoot me for no reason at all. I'm not goin' to stand here and listen to any more of this crazy talk."

He tried to turn and push his way through the crowd still packed in behind him. But the mob didn't budge. They wouldn't let Galloway through. They stood there, staring at him coldly. One of them said, "Let's have a look at that proof, Marshal."

Dillon stood a few feet away from Galloway. He said, "In the loot stolen from Jeff Foster were a lot of silver dollars. Some of them were left behind with the small amount of greenbacks the killer buried where it would be easily found on Gant's place, to throw more suspicion on Jan Gant. He probably left them there because silver dollars —a lot of them—are heavy. And he already had as many as he could carry. Anyhow, we still have some of Uncle Jeff's silver dollars. The killer has the rest of them. If we can match up the ones he has with the others, prove they *all* belonged to Uncle Jeff Foster, we—"

"How you going to do anything like that?" Galloway demanded. "All silver dollars look the same."

"Do they, Galloway? Maybe—if you don't look at them

too closely. . . . There's something you don't know, Mike Galloway. Uncle Jeff kept those silver dollars for a purpose. He planned to use them as a trap that would catch the thief, in case some day his money was stolen. You didn't know about that, did you, Galloway?"

Galloway looked as though he had aged ten years in the past few minutes.

"Those silver dollars were all marked, Galloway. On each one Uncle Jeff Foster cut his initials in letters so small and so well-hidden on the coin that they could not be detected, except under close examination. But those initials are there on each coin."

"No! No, they're not, I tell you!" Galloway cried.

"How do you know, Mike," one of the men in the crowd behind him asked, "if you've never seen those cartwheels?"

"I—I—well, I don't, really. What I meant was that this whole thing is just a big pack of lies. Dillon can't prove one word of it. All right, maybe the silver dollars he found were marked—maybe the others are too. But what does that prove? *I* don't have them!"

"Don't you, Galloway?"

Galloway turned to the crowd behind him. "We'll go to my place and let the Marshal tear it apart and see if he can find that missing loot. Some of you can go as witnesses. If he finds a penny of that money, I'll put my own neck in the noose. Isn't that fair enough?"

"It would be, if the money was hidden at your place, Galloway," Dillon continued. "There are other places you could hide it. You might even have it with you."

Galloway laughed. "That much money? Now I know you're loco, Marshal. My pocket would be bulging, with that much money. Especially with a lot of it in silver."

Smiling grimly, Dillon held out his right hand. "Galloway, my knuckles are still a little swollen from hitting you in the stomach earlier today. That punch hurt my hand bad. I wonder why? It shouldn't hurt that way, hitting a man in the stomach. At first I thought perhaps I'd hit your belt buckle. Then I saw that you weren't wearing a belt, Galloway—at least not the regular kind. Anyhow, I didn't think much more about it at the time. But a little while ago, while I was trying to figure what you might have done with that stolen money, my sore knuckles gave me the answer. . . . You know what I'm talking about, don't you, Mike?"

"No!" Galloway shouted. He spread out his arms and tried to push back into the crowd behind him. Somebody

roughly shoved him forward again.

"No, Marshal, no!" Galloway repeated.

"You're wearing a money belt, Galloway. You're carrying Uncle Jeff's stolen cash spread out in that belt around your middle. You have some of those silver dollars tucked into the front of the money belt. That's what I hit with my fist, Galloway—good, hard, old silver coin of the realm!"

Now Galloway was fumbling under his shirt.

"That's right, Mike. Take the money belt off and hand it to me." Dillon held out his hand.

Chester moved forward and stood next to Dillon. Grinning, he said, "Good grief, Mr. Dillon, how'd you ever happen to figure out something like that?"

Watching Galloway's trembling hands fumbling under his shirt, undoing the money belt, Dillon said, "There just wasn't any other answer, Chester, when I knew for sure Galloway was our man and I thought about what could have hurt my fist that way."

Someone in the crowd behind Galloway shouted, "I'm convinced now. It was Galloway all the time, all right. And the dirty skunk was tryin' to get us to lynch an innocent man! Well, I say we ought to give Galloway some of his own medicine. Marshal, I say we ought to hang Mike Galloway!"

Dillon answered sharply, "That's about what I'd expect of men who'd let Galloway make them part of a lynch mob. Now you turn on your own leader!"

"But, Marshal, we—"

"I've heard all the talk about hanging I want to hear right now," Dillon said, cutting him off. "From here on the law's going to take its proper course. All I want from the rest of you is to disband and get out of here. I'll handle Galloway. . . . Chester, go let Mr. Gant out of that cell. We've got a brand-new guest ready to use it—a man who's learned the hard way that the end of the crime road is a dead-end one."

"Yes, sir, Mr. Dillon." Chester reached for the ring of keys on his belt and turned toward the cell.

"You're right, Marshal," Galloway said in a subdued voice. "You've got me dead to rights, with this stolen money on me. No sense in my tryin' to talk my way out any more."

He had the money belt unstrapped from about his waist, and he pulled it out from under his shirt. The belt was made of heavy canvas webbing, with slotlike pockets all around it to hold money. Those pockets were bulging with cash, but they had not shown under the looseness of the man's shirt where it billowed out a little from the waist.

As Dillon reached for the money belt, Mike Galloway suddenly swung it in a savage, whipping sweep. Dillon ducked but still the belt hit him a glancing blow and knocked him off balance. At the same time, in the follow-through, it cracked down hard across the gun Dillon held in his right hand. It knocked the gun from his grasp.

Galloway jumped forward, away from the reach of the men behind him. He drew his own Frontier Colt and covered the whole group. Crouched, his face a snarling mask, he was like a rabid animal at bay.

"You were wrong, Marshal," he said. "The road isn't dead-end for me yet. There's still this little detour. . . . Don't any of you try to stop me from getting out of here. I've killed two men. You won't be able to hang me any higher for killing a few more."

Chester, back by the cell, had set his shotgun down to open the door for Jan Gant. Now he started to make a move toward the gun. Galloway swung the Colt toward him.

"Don't do it, Chester!" he said.

"He's right, Chester, don't try anything." Dillon glanced

quickly at the men crowded into the doorway. "Don't any of you try to stop him, either. Let him go."

"That's smart talk, Marshal," Galloway said.

He started to edge toward the rear exit of the building.

"I'm goin' out the back door. When I get to the hallway that leads to it, I'm going to walk backwards, facing this way. The first man that tries to come down that hallway after me is a dead man."

Nobody said anything. They all just stood there, unmoving, as Galloway edged toward the rear hallway.

"And even after you hear that back door slam shut, don't come after me," Galloway said. "I'll be looking at that door. I'll shoot anyone that tries to get out of it."

He backed out of sight into the rear passageway.

They heard his footsteps as he moved cautiously backward. They heard the door creak open and then slam shut again.

17   *Shoot-Out*

At the sound of that rear door closing, there was a stir of activity from the crowd who had been with Galloway. One of them shouted, "Let's go get him! If we catch up with him, before he can find a horse—"

"Hold it, all of you," Dillon commanded. He held up a warning hand. "If you men go after Galloway, some of you will get killed. Besides, I'd rather take him alive, if I can. This is still a job for law officers. Chester and I'll handle it."

Chester stepped forward, holding a rifle at ready. "What you want me to do, Mr. Dillon? We'd better move fast."

"I know. Chester, you go out the front and head for the livery stable a few doors down from here on Front Street."

"I know where you mean, Mr. Dillon. You think he'll go there?"

"Either there or the one up the other direction on the

street behind the jailhouse. I'll go cover that one."

"All right, Mr. Dillon."

"Chester!"

"Yes, sir?"

"Be careful. Galloway's got nothing to lose and everything to gain by shooting to kill. Stick close to the buildings as you move toward that stable."

"Yes, sir. I surely will, Mr. Dillon."

Then, as Chester hurried out the front door, Dillon moved fast toward the rear of the building. When he reached the back door, he kicked it open with his foot and stood back, his gun cocked and ready as he stared out into the darkness.

Nothing happened. Dillon stepped outside. He turned right and walked fast toward the lantern hanging outside the livery stable in the next block. He was fairly certain that Galloway would try to get a horse at that one first. He would hardly take a chance on a main thoroughfare such as Front Street. That was why Dillon had chosen this direction for his own pursuit of the killer. If possible, he wanted the satisfaction of nailing Mike Galloway personally. He felt as though the thing between them was almost a personal affair.

Near the livery now, Dillon hugged the shadows and kept his forty-four trained on the doorway of the stable. At any moment he expected to see Galloway come riding out. But nothing happened.

Dillon stepped inside the dimly lit livery and saw only a heavy-set, muscular man, wearing a blacksmith's apron, working over a forge. The man looked up at Dillon, surprised.

"Howdy, Marshal," he said. "What you doin', prowlin' around here with your gun in hand? Lookin' for burglars?" The man laughed heartily. "Well, I ain't seen any lately. Ain't much to steal around here."

Before Dillon could answer, there was the rattling sound of distant gunfire from the direction of Front Street. The Marshal knew that he had guessed wrong.

Swiftly he ran out of the livery, raced down an alley between buildings, and came out onto Front Street. From the direction of the livery where Dillon had sent Chester, there was the orange flash of gunfire from the dark shadows. About fifty feet away, on the other side of the street, an answering shot sent a jagged spurt of flame against the darkness.

Flattened against a side of a building as he moved in that

direction, Dillon shouted, "Hold it, Chester! Wait until I get there!"

There was no answer. The whole of Dodge City seemed suddenly as silent as a ghost town. Down the street as far as Dillon could see there was not a human being in sight. That was the way it was when shooting broke out on the street. Everybody darted out of the way into the nearest place that offered any protection—into shallow doorways, into the mouths of alleys.

Dillon kept moving forward. He reached the jailhouse and went on past it. Then, as he passed a darkened doorway, one of the men who had been in the Galloway mob whispered, "Chester is up on the veranda of the next building, Marshal. He took cover behind some barrels. He's pinned Mike down about fifty feet farther on, the other side of the street. Mike's turned a horse trough over and is barricaded behind it. He's goin' to be mighty hard to get at there."

"Yeah," Dillon answered.

"Marshal?"

"What is it?"

"Chester may have been hit. I ain't heard him movin' around the last few minutes."

"Uh-huh." Dillon sounded choked up. "That's what I was afraid of."

From behind the water trough down the street, gunfire flashed again. The clap-sound of the shot echoed back and forth between buildings. Wood splintered on the side of the building where Chester was.

Dillon aimed and fired twice in the direction of the gun flash. Then he said to the man in the doorway, "What happened before I got here?"

"Mike Galloway got himself a horse in that stable. He came ridin' out of there, full tilt, shooting at Chester and the rest of us. Then Chester cut loose a shot, and the way it looked to me, he grazed one of the horse's legs. Anyhow, the mount stumbled and threw Galloway and kept on going. Mike, he didn't seem hurt too bad. He rolled over behind that trough, after tipping it over. He and Chester started wingin' shots at each other."

"Thanks." Dillon glided through the darkness and climbed up on the veranda of the building where Chester was. It was pitch black there in the shadows. Dillon whispered, "Chester! Chester, you all right?"

There was no answer.

Dillon moved forward cautiously, feeling his way in

front of him with his free hand. Then his hand touched
the cloth of a shirt. "Chester!" he said again.

His hand moved until it found Chester's face. It moved
up to his temple and Dillon knew then why Chester didn't
answer. His hand felt the wet stickiness of blood. Chester
had been hit, all right.

Dillon straightened up, trying to get control of his emo-
tions, trying to keep himself from rushing blindly toward
Mike Galloway and killing him with his bare hands for
doing this to Chester.

Another shot flared from behind the water trough. The
lead *thucked* into the wall only a few feet from Dillon's
head. He ducked and scuttled along the wall, reached the
end of the veranda, and stepped off onto the plank walk.
Then he dropped down until he was sprawled flat in the
dust of the street. He began to wriggle forward.

Dillon knew that there wasn't much sense in wasting
more lead, firing at a man barricaded as well as Galloway
was. His only chance was to get down there, even with
Galloway or a little past him, on this side of the street. That
way he would have an open shot at the man.

The next moment Galloway fired again. When the echo
of the shot died out, he yelled, "I can't see you, Chester—

or Dillon—whoever it is. But I can hear you. I know what you're doin'. You're crawlin' along the street, tryin' to get behind me. It won't work though. I can shoot at the sound of you. I'll get you first."

There was another shot, and it dug up dust and dirt a couple of feet from Dillon's nose. He kept wriggling forward through the dust.

Up ahead, a small swatch of light, falling from a lamp-lit window, cut across the street. Dillon had to get through that, somehow. For a moment, while he was crossing it, he knew he would be a bright target. But there was no way around it.

Mike Galloway had his eyes on that fall of light across the road too. He was running short of ammunition. He knew that this was his one chance to get whoever was stalking him. He peered out around the edge of the trough, his Colt Frontier Model trained on that sprawl of light. He saw a figure start to crawl hurriedly through it. He aimed and fired. There was a grunting sound. The legs of the crawling man remained in the patch of light. They didn't move.

Galloway slowly got to his feet, crouched, and took dead aim at where the rest of that body would be. He

wasn't going to take any chances on his being only wounded.

But before he could shoot again, there was a jet of orange flame from Dillon's forty-four.

Galloway dropped his Frontier Colt. He clasped both hands over his stomach, bent forward, and crumpled into the dirt.

Dillon got up and ran toward him. He grabbed Galloway's gun. Other men ran up and joined him, and somebody came out of one of the buildings carrying a lantern. A man said to Dillon, "I thought you'd been shot, Marshal. I thought he got you when you moved through that slat of lamplight."

"So did Galloway. That's what I wanted him to think, so he'd get up nerve enough to get out from behind that barricade for a moment."

Another man said, looking down at Galloway, "He got out of it too quickly, too easily, Marshal, considering everything he's done."

"Maybe not," Dillon said. He stepped toward Galloway and rolled him over with his foot. He looked down at the hole in Galloway's shirt, just above the waistline. There was no blood there.

Dillon bent and opened Galloway's shirt. He poked at the dent in the money belt and pulled out a badly bent and dented silver dollar.

"The same coins that got him into trouble saved his life —for a while," Dillon said. "I knew he took that money belt with him. I figured he'd have strapped it on again. It made a good target. . . . There! He's beginning to come to. I think he'll live until the law decides otherwise."

Dillon straightened up and handed Galloway's Colt to one of the others. "Keep him covered with this and herd him back to the jail building. I've got to go and see about Chester."

Before Dillon could turn around, a voice behind him said, "Don't you worry about ol' Chester none, Mr. Dillon. It takes more than a little nick at the temple to keep a good man down."

Relief showing on his troubled face, Dillon wheeled around. Grinning, he said, "Why, you lazy son of a gun, I should have known you were just fakin', slackin' off until all the work was over."

Then Dillon took a closer look at the wound at Chester's temple. "That looks like more than a nick, Chester." He shook his head wonderingly. "You must have more lives than a cat. We'd better get you to Doc Adams and let him take a look at it."

"Oh, it ain't all that bad, Mr. Dillon. But if you say so. . . ."

Prodding Mike Galloway in front of them, then, they moved up the street toward the jailhouse.

18   *All Quiet*

"There's one thing more I don't understand, Mr. Dillon," Chester said a little later, as they sat in Doc Adams' office while Doc dressed the wound on Chester's head.

"What's that, Chester?"

"Well, you told Galloway that those silver dollars had been marked by Uncle Jeff Foster. I looked 'em all over mighty closely, Mr. Dillon. I couldn't find any trace of where he'd cut his initials into those coins."

Dillon grinned. "Do you always believe everything you hear, Chester?"

Chester's eyes widened. "You mean you just made that up, Mr. Dillon?"

"Why not? I figured Galloway sure wouldn't know whether it was true or not and that it would trip him up into maybe making a slip of the tongue, admitting that he had some of those stolen coins."

"Well, I declare!" Chester said, shaking his head.

"Consarn it, man, can't you sit still while somebody's tryin' to patch up your fool head?" Doc Adams scolded Chester.

For a moment nobody said anything. Then Chester's throat and lips moved faintly but no sound seemed to come from his mouth. At the same time, though, another voice, similar to Chester's but strange and high-pitched, came from behind Adams.

"Doc, you're the sourest ol' apple that ever grew on the tree! You stay so mad at the world, it's a wonder you don't bite your own self out of pure meanness!"

Doc Adams jerked back, looking startled. "Eh, what's that?" He turned around, looking behind him, a puzzled expression on his face.

Chester and Marshal Dillon broke out laughing. Chester said, hardly able to control himself long enough to speak, "It was me, Doc. It was me! Just a little trick of ventriloquism I picked up from one of those pamphlets. . . . You told me to learn it and amaze my friends. Well, didn't it amaze you, Doc?"

"Oh, shut up!" Doc said, blushing. "Most childish thing

I ever heard of a grown man tryin' to do."

Marshal Dillon, standing by Doc Adams' desk, reached down and picked up a small, cheaply printed pamphlet. He said, "What's this, Doc? Here's one of those pamphlets I didn't notice before. It's called 'Secret Exercises to Make You Feel Young Again.'"

Doc Adams wheeled around. "I—I just needed somethin' to read, that's all. You don't think I—Matt Dillon, you stay out of my personal papers!"

But Chester and the Marshal were laughing too hard even to hear him. . . .

A few blocks away at Mrs. Biddy McCue's rooming house, Jan Gant and Tommy sat on the edge of Mrs. Gant's bed. Each of them held one of her pale hands. Color was beginning to show in Mrs. Gant's face again and her eyes were beginning to brighten. She was too weak to do anything except smile.

Now that the first greetings were over, this family, together for the first time in many years, didn't seem to have much to say. But then, this was one of those times when words didn't have much value. It was enough for the time being that they were all together once more.

Outside, the dusty streets of Dodge City were quiet once again. The night was almost over. The townspeople settled down to sleep while the moon and the stars shone gently overhead.